The Preacher's Dear

The Preacher's Dear

Sparks Fly as
City and Country
Collide

A Novel

Dwight Burkholder

ISBN 13: 978-1-4675-0551-2
Library of Congress Catalog Card Number: 2010905182

Chapter 1

Jim Black sat at his desk, his head in his hands. He had just preached a sermon on the grace of God. At the end of the service, as people filed out past him, several people from different families had said, "Yes, the grace of God is good, but we cannot have a twenty-years-behind-bars individual in our congregation. No way!"

Jim's temples throbbed. He rubbed them gently with his fingers, realizing that if it wasn't for the grace of God we would all be lost. The sermon he had preached that morning had been timely; something he felt God had wanted him to do. It was a message God had led him to preach, and he had preached his heart out trying to help people understand that we are all sinners saved by grace—that we're all human.

Three families had voiced their concerns. They spoke of leaving the church because they wanted no part of a fellowship where they would be afraid—afraid for their family; afraid of what people would say. How could he help satisfy the needs of his church congregation?

Jim felt frustration, anger and pity. He was angry that people would judge a man when they didn't know who he was; a man who had been incarcerated for twenty years; a man who accepted Christ three years before going to prison; a man who, while in a drunken stupor, had committed a terrible crime years before he had found a church family. Through the love of neighbors and the invitation of friends, this man, Ernest, and his wife had found Jim's church. They started attending and found peace and acceptance in the congregation. Ernest had found that peace because he realized that he was a sinner. Both he and his wife had given their hearts to the Lord. The glow of Jesus on their faces left little doubt about their relationship with Christ. How they drank in His words; how they grew.

Ernest had confessed his sins to the pastor in confidence, and the congregation, not knowing about his past, had accepted him. Then everything had caught up with him. For twenty years Ernest served his prison time, and now, in just a couple of weeks, he would be set free. His natural desire was to go to Jim's church. But now people knew who he was. They knew his past. God, in His grace, had completely erased the sins of Ernest's past, but the humans within the church had fears—fear for their own family; fear of what could be repeated.

The older members of the congregation who knew Ernest had no fear. They knew who he was, and they knew his walk. Jim, himself, had been to see him often in prison and had marveled and praised God at the way Ernest had kept his faith throughout his incarceration.

Jim glanced at the clock on the wall. He had an appointment—one he looked forward to the way kids look forward to Christmas. Tomorrow was the first day of deer hunting season in Pennsylvania. Every year, he and his two buddies got together in their hunting camp and enjoyed several days of camaraderie, hunting, fun and feasting. Oh, the enjoyment of being together.

Jim was already packed and ready to go. He dreamed, with anticipation, about the tree that he would sit in. He had hunted that same spot year after year, and year after year he had seen a lot of deer. Just as Christmas never gets old, for Jim, deer hunting never got old. The venison it provided, which was always a blessing, was healthy meat to last the family all year.

Yes, hunting provided meat to feed the family. All through high school, college and seminary, Jim had lived at home with his parents and provided his family with meat. But now, having moved into his own home eight months ago, he had his own freezer. Jim dreamed of the time when his own wife would get the meat out of the freezer and have supper waiting for him when he returned home from work each day. He dreamed of when he would have children. As they grew, he would share with them and teach them the joys of hunting and being in God's nature.

Jim rubbed his temples with his hands again and breathed a prayer. "God, direct my thoughts, direct my actions and direct my life. Let me be Your vessel so that others can see You through me."

Suddenly, a bubbling of enthusiasm from way down deep caused his face to break out in a grin. His duties were over for the day, and he was off the clock, so to speak. This afternoon, Pastor Burns, the senior pastor, and his wife would be returning home from their vacation, and Jim had the next three days free. He was free to go to Pennsylvania; free to hunt with his friends. In an hour, he was scheduled to meet with his cousins to make the four-hour trip to the cabin in Pennsylvania. There, they would meet with their other friends and spend the three days together. It was time to go hunting. Pastor Burns could handle the church and its conflict.

Jim walked out to his Jeep Cherokee parked in the church parking lot. His six-foot frame easily slid into the driver's seat. Mentally, he began to run over his checklist: gun, bullets, knife, tree stand, boots, wrap, rain gear. He looked up and squinted. He certainly wouldn't need the rain gear. *Hunting in the rain is good,* he thought, *but when a man doesn't have to hunt in the rain, that is even better.*

Jim started the engine and began to head out to his cousins' house. Suddenly, his stomach growled, and he realized that he was hungry. He looked down at his watch.

In forty-five minutes, he was supposed to meet with his cousins.

Ah, yes, spending time with the cousins. Andrea was Jim's first cousin. She had married George Jackson, and they owned a small grocery store in town. George was Jim's hunting buddy, and they loved to hunt and spend time together. Andrea was the type of lady whom Jim had set as a benchmark for the type of woman that he prayed God would bless him with someday. Her qualities, her spirituality, her beauty . . . Jim had been awfully proud and thankful when God had brought Andrea and George together. Now he was best friends with the couple, and his relationship with them had created an offshoot family with whom he felt comfortable and could relax. When he was with those two, he felt like he was at home.

Jim glanced down at his watch again, and then looked up and saw a Burger King. He decided that a Whopper with cheese and a small drink would be just right. He didn't want to eat too much, because supper that evening would be in the cabin—the evening before hunting season began. He thought about the festivities they would have, the bantering they would enjoy, the stories they would swap. Jim's enthusiasm grew. Oh, this was a good time of year!

Jim swung into the Burger King and parked the car. Drive-thrus were a symbol of a fast-paced world, and he wanted to slow down and relax. He went in and ordered, thanking God in a silent prayer for the food, for the time of year, for the fun, and for the excitement. Yes, life was good.

However, he realized that he needed to pray for other things, too—for the congregation, for the growth of those who were babes in Christ, for those who needed to see that they were forgiven and that they needed to be able to forgive people--even people like Ernest. He also needed to pray for his future spouse; the evenings were lonely and long. As he finished his prayer, he grinned. The next several days would certainly not be lonely. The next several days would offer some of the highlights of his year.

Jim gobbled down his sandwich and got a refill on his drink. He left the restaurant, jumped back into his Jeep, and looked at his watch again. In just fifteen minutes, he would be at George and Andrea's. They would be ready to throw their things into the Jeep—their gear, the food, the other supplies they would need on the trip—and they would be on their way. Jim felt lighthearted. He rolled his eyes toward heaven and smiled. "Thank You, God," he said, "for the rest of today."

Andrea was excited. She and George had left church as soon as they could, following Jim's benediction, and now they were home. She was all packed, but she still had to put the perishables in the two coolers. She wanted to wait until the last minute to do that, so in the meantime she had put their hunting gear together. She and George had stayed up until midnight the night before going through their list to make sure they had everything: guns, ammo, knives, the tree stand, boots, wrap, clothes, all the hunting accessories, rattle horns, buck calls, buck lures.

Now they were all ready to go except for the coolers, and loading them up would take only a couple of minutes. Andrea thought of her husband, George and how he was looking forward so much to this trip. George was overworked, and this trip would give him a couple of days away from the grocery store. Andrea knew how much this trip meant to him—the escape from the responsibilities, pressures and headaches brought on by the daily grind. Andrea knew the love that George had for hunting. No, it wasn't just about killing an animal; it was about the fun, the camaraderie of being with friends, the thrill and passion of sitting quietly in the woods, taking in nature and watching the squirrels, deer, turkeys, birds and the chipmunks. George loved being able to rise to the challenge of outwitting a whitetail buck.

As Andrea thought of George, her mind drifted to Jim. He was her favorite cousin. Jim and George could be brothers. Their hearts seemed to beat as one for their love of the outdoors and hunting. Andrea knew the anticipation, the excitement and the emotional fever that interwove her husband and cousin together in what they enjoyed doing. Yes, tomorrow was the first day of Pennsylvania's hunting season, and each day leading up to opening day was a build-up of expectancy and enthusiasm.

Andrea laughed, thinking of all the "opening days" that Jim and George had hoped to share again this year. The first Saturday of October had been the opening day for bow season in Virginia. This was followed by the opening day of muzzleloader season in Virginia on the first Saturday of November. The third Saturday of November in Virginia was the opening day of rifle season. Tomorrow, the Monday after Thanksgiving, was the opening day of rifle season in Pennsylvania. Andrea chuckled. Every time she turned around there was another "opening day." But she didn't mind. She enjoyed the thrill and excitement of this time of year.

Andrea chuckled to herself. George was a lucky man—no, a blessed man—to have a wife who enjoyed the out of doors, the camaraderie of the hunting season, the thrill of excitement of harvested game, and the meat that the harvest provided. Andrea glanced at the clock and looked around to find George. Jim would arrive in fifteen to twenty minutes, and he would be just as excited as if this were his first hunt. Andrea's own demeanor was predictably contentment with happy anticipation.

Andrea went back to her bedroom. Yes, she was also packed and ready, and she had her own gun, a .270 rifle. But this year, she also had a secret: she had bought her own

Pennsylvania hunting license without George's knowledge of it. Although the women were in charge of cooking the meals, there was plenty of time for her to relax and enjoy the cabin experience. On more than one occasion, she had hiked out behind the cabin and sat in the woods and relaxed. And more than once she had wished she'd had her own rifle and license, because she had seen legal bucks—ones with horns, three points on either side. The men would hunt all day and not get a thing, yet she had found a little funnel created by a narrow strip of mountain laurel bushes that ran perpendicular across several small mountain ridges where the bucks often appeared. The deer liked the comfort of the natural camouflage, as it provided a safe means of travel through the open woods. Secretly, Andrea dreamed of being able to gloat; to call and announce her happy news on the walkie-talkies; to have her deer already hanging up on the meat pole when the men came in from a long day of hunting. She giggled to herself. The trick was going to be getting her gun and ammo into the Jeep without the men noticing it. She would think of something. She didn't know how, but she knew that she could do it in a way that would preserve her surprise.

Andrea was just finishing loading the coolers when the phone rang. "Who would be calling now?" she said to herself as she looked at the phone. She blew a wisp of hair out of her face, pulled it back with one hand, and reached for the phone with the other. She answered it on the third ring.

"Andrea! You're home!" the voice on the other end exclaimed.

Andrea immediately recognized the voice. It was Susan Handley, her college roommate who had gone through nursing school with her. They were close, though not the closest of buddies. Susan lived in Ohio. Her husband had been killed in a car accident two years earlier, and she had struggled emotionally and spiritually trying to learn how to cope and how to survive. Susan still had bitterness hanging over her and, at times, depression. She was still seeking for answers and living in the past.

Andrea glanced at the clock, knowing Jim would be arriving very soon. George was carrying all of the supplies, the tubs of clothing and his gun out onto their porch so that when Jim arrived, they could quickly load the Jeep and be on their way. Like her, George's enthusiasm for the trip was bubbling over. These were the days that he looked forward to every year.

Andrea sighed. This was not the time to get a phone call from Susan. She knew that talking to Susan could take time—time that she didn't have right now. Yet she also knew that she couldn't turn a deaf ear to her friend.

"Andrea," Susan said. "I'm glad you answered the phone. I need to talk to you."

"Yes, Susan, I'm here," Andrea replied. "I'm glad you called. What's up?"

"It's getting to be that time of year again," Susan said. "You know, this week it will be two years, and . . . and I have to get away from the memories, from the pain."

"Well, that's good, Susan. You need to stay busy and do things. But you can't always run from reality."

"Yes, I know," Susan said. "But I need a break. I need to get away . . . to get into a different environment so I can breathe. I lie in bed at night and feel as though I'm being strangled. It's so hard to . . . to let go. It's hard to get up in the morning and put my best face on and meet the day. I still ask why, and at times I cry at night."

As Andrea listened, a sense of pity came over her. Life for her was so full and exciting. Yet the anguish that her friend was feeling . . . she paused, trying to comprehend, in a heartbeat, the agony that Susan was going through.

"So, if you're getting away, Susan, where are you going? What are you doing? Where are you going to find your new environment?"

"Andrea, I'm coming to see you. I need to spend some time with you."

Andrea watched as George carried another box outside onto the porch. "When . . . are you coming, Susan? We are busy, but we'd love to see you. Our schedules are full, but I will make time for you—you know that. So, when are you coming? When will you be here? We would love to spend some time with you."

There was a pause on the phone. "Susan," Andrea asked, "are you there?"

"Yes, I'm here," Susan said quietly. "But I'm also *here*."

"Here?" Andrea asked. "Where is . . . here?"

"Give me thirty seconds, Andrea, and I'll be in your driveway."

"What?"

"I didn't call ahead of time. I just needed to come."

"Susan, you're *here*?" Andrea rubbed her hands through her hair.

George came in through the door. Hearing a vehicle driving into the lane, he looked back, thinking it would be Jim. A frown crossed his face when he realized it was a strange car with a woman in it. *Who would that be?* he thought. "Somebody's here," he said to Andrea.

Andrea held her hand over the receiver so that Susan couldn't hear. "It's Susan Handley—she's here to see us. What are we going to do?"

George looked out the window at the car, then at Susan, and then at Andrea. "Well, dear," he said, "I'm going hunting!"

"What am I going to do, George?" Andrea said. "I want to go, too."

"Well, I certainly expect you to come with me," George replied. "Tell Susan it doesn't suit until Wednesday evening."

"George, we can't do that! She's a friend, she's depressed, and she needs our help."

George rolled his eyes. *Now what?* he wondered. He had been looking forward to this trip for ages—it was the highlight of his whole year—and the last thing he needed was for his plans to be derailed. Frustration crept into his face as he looked out the window and saw Susan getting out of her car. He looked back to Andrea. "Well, hang up the phone and go to the door, because she's coming in."

Andrea stared at George with a questioning look on her face. George shrugged and picked up the last tub of clothing to be placed on the porch. Andrea went and opened the door. "Susan," she said. "It's so good to see you. Come in, come in!"

Susan was modestly dressed in jeans and a light sweater. She was a pretty woman, five foot six, with brown hair that hung to her shoulders. She had eyes that were so many different shades of brown that when people looked into them, they had to stare to find all the many dimensions of color that were deep within them.

In her college days, Susan had been a happy-go-lucky girl who was energetic and full of life. She always looked for the positive and for something to be cheerful and excited about. When she had graduated from nursing school and gone back home to marry her childhood sweetheart, her life had felt complete. Then, two years ago, a phone call had changed her life forever. The officer told her that someone had been in a hurry and had gambled on a yellow light, broadsiding her husband's car on the driver's side. Her husband had never had a chance. Now, Susan merely existed. She never clearly thought through how her actions might affect other people. In this instance, she never wondered if it suited George and Andrea for her to come. She just came.

Susan approached the door and, glancing the hunting gear and food, suddenly realized that she had made a blunder. "Oh, Andrea," she said. "You're going away."

Andrea embraced Susan and gave her a big hug. "Hi, Susan, it's so good to see you. It has been almost two years. I wish you had called earlier. Maybe we could have made arrangements. We could have set a time. We are going hunting for several days."

Susan looked helpless as she realized the situation that her unannounced arrival had thrust upon her friend. "Oh! I guess . . ." she stammered, as the reality of her rash travel planning jolted whatever emotionally frayed senses she had left, "I guess I can go to a hotel for several days. I didn't think. I just came. What should I do?"

Andrea looked at George, and George looked at Andrea. "You can't do that to her, Andrea," he said. "If she needs a friend—if she needs to talk—there'll be plenty of time at the cabin for you ladies to spend together."

Andrea looked back at George. "Is there room?" she asked. "What will Jim think? What will the others think—Sam and Martha? Will we have enough food?"

George laughed. "We'll have plenty of food, and we're going to get more."

"We only have three bedrooms," Andrea replied. "One for us, one for Sam and Martha, and one for Jim."

"There's a couch," George said. "She can sleep on the couch."

Susan was listening and quickly picked up the conversation. "I can sleep anywhere," she said. "The couch will be fine. Oh, may I come? I so desperately need to be near you, Andrea."

A million thoughts whirled through Andrea's head. This was the first year that she was going hunting herself—although George didn't know it. She had made her plans, and now those plans would be disrupted. Instead of hunting, she would be friend-sitting. She had paid more than 100 dollars for her hunting license. That would be a waste of money!

Realizing that there was nothing to be done, Andrea brightened and said, "By all means, come with us."

Susan smiled, and then looked again at the gear and the wrap. A frown quickly passed over her face. "You're going to a cabin?" she said. "You're going hunting? You're going to kill Bambi?"

George grinned. "No, not Bambi," he said. "We're going to kill Bambi's granddaddy. I just happen to know where he is. I have him all figured out."

"Oh, my," Susan said. "You can't kill any deer. Why, they're so pretty."

George glanced at Andrea with a question mark on his brows. "Yes, Susan," he said, "we're going hunting, and yes, deer are God's wonderful creatures. They're wonderful and beautiful to watch. They're also wonderful to try to outsmart, wonderful to harvest, and wonderful to eat. Deer are a part of life—the same as any other life, any other cycle—and yes, we're going hunting, and yes, we hope to harvest deer. It's something you need to accept if you want to come along with us. You can choose to go or stay in a motel, but we would welcome you to come along. We are going to a hunting cabin, though, and yes, we do expect to be successful."

Susan put her hand to her mouth, quickly realizing that she could be an unwelcome guest or an invited guest. It was up to her to create the tenor and atmosphere of the next several days. She knew that people hunted, and though she wasn't familiar or comfortable with it, she believed that she could endure it.

"Okay," she said. "I'll go."

At that instant, there was a honking in the driveway, and all eyes turned in that direction. There was Jim in his Jeep. Jim opened the door and bounded out, running up the stairs. "Okay, George, Andrea, let's go! Let's get this day rolling!" Just then, he stopped. Something wasn't right. There was another woman standing beside Andrea. This could delay their departure time.

"Jim," said Andrea, "this is Susan Handley. She and I went through nursing school together. She showed up ten minutes ahead of you and wanted to spend some time with us, so she's going along on the hunting trip, too."

Jim looked at Susan. Red flags were going up in his brain, but something about her made it hard for him not to stare. She was beautiful—and her eyes! Jim tried not to look, but he couldn't draw his eyes away from hers. There was such depth in those eyes.

"Susan," he said, "glad to meet you. I'm Jim. Jim Black."

"Reverend Jim Black," George said.

Susan started to shake Jim's hand, but then shrunk back when George said "Reverend." "You're God's man?" she blurted out. "You promote a God who kills? Who lets people die?"

"No," Jim said. "I am God's man, but God is in control. God has a plan for each of us."

"Susan lost her husband two years ago in a car wreck," Andrea said.

"I'm sorry," Jim said. "That is a grief that is hard to bear. I'm truly sorry."

"So am I . . . so am I," Susan murmured.

"Well," said Andrea, "if you're going along, Susan, throw your suitcase in the Jeep. I'll grab a few more of our camouflage coats. I have an extra pair of boots; we're about the same size. That will give you something to wear so you can be more rustic and feel more at home in the cabin environment. And, yes . . . a sleeping bag. We need a sleeping bag."

Again, the disappointing thought crossed Andrea's mind: *Would she get to go hunting if Susan was there? Would she have to sacrifice her own desires and hopes and plans?* In answer to her concerns, an idea suddenly came into her head the way a light bulb comes on when flipping the switch. "Susan," she said, "help me while the men start loading the Jeep. You can put your suitcase on the porch for them to pack. Then come with me, and we'll find you a sleeping bag and gather the rest of my things."

Susan quickly retrieved her suitcase from her car and set it on the porch. She hurried back into the house.

"I'm back here!" Andrea hollered. "Help me, Susan."

Susan went back to the master bedroom. When she entered the room, Andrea looked up with a grin on her face. "There may be a surprise or two this year," she said. "The men don't know everything. Here. Help me hide my gun in this sleeping bag, and this ammo, too."

"What . . . what are you doing, Andrea?" Susan asked.

"I may go hunting myself, and I don't want the men to know. This will be our secret. Not a word. This gives me a way to have the gun hidden and get it into camp."

Andrea and Susan quickly took the gun and wrapped it in the sleeping bag. Andrea stuck some ammo into her pants pockets, and they carried the sleeping bag out to the Jeep. The men had just finished packing, and they made room for the sleeping bag. "No," Andrea said. "We women can pack this."

Jim looked into Susan's eyes, the different hues of brown, again, causing him to stare. Susan returned his glance, and then, lowering her eyelids, turned and helped Andrea put the sleeping bag, with the hidden gun in it, into the back of the Jeep. "Are we ready?" Jim asked. "Let's roll. Sam and Martha will be looking for us four hours from now. They'll have supper ready—vegetable deer soup." It would taste good.

Suddenly, Susan felt a bit shy. She looked at Andrea, and Andrea looked at George. "George," Andrea said, "you have long legs. Why don't you sit up front next to Jim? We ladies will hold the back down."

George immediately sensed what was going on. He looked over at Jim and saw the relief on his face. Susan saw the relief on Jim's face as well, and when she did, the irritation bubbled up from within her. Maybe she was impulsive, and maybe she had messed up their plans, but she wasn't poison. Yet as she glanced at George and Andrea, she realized the problems she was creating. When she and her husband had been married, they had been close and had done practically everything together, so to have Andrea and George separated just didn't seem like the right thing to do.

With a slight shake of her head and with grim determination, Susan climbed into the back seat with Andrea. "I'm sorry again, Andrea, for my impulsiveness. I hope I'm not creating too many problems. I hope you all can have the fun that you normally do. I'll be as quiet as a little mouse and a flower on the wall."

"Come now, Susan," Andrea said, putting her hand down on Susan's. "These are some of the best days of our lives. We enjoy it very, very much, and we look forward to having you along. In fact, you're going to have a couple of the best days of your life. Enjoy it and take it all in. We are going to have fun!"

Chapter 2

The ride up Interstate 81 was uneventful except for a lot of light bantering. Jim and George kept talking about how big a buck they would kill. Andrea and Susan merrily chitchatted about a number of things. Overall, there was a festive mood in the Jeep as Jim kept it moving north, heading into Pennsylvania.

As Jim was talking to George, he kept sneaking peeks back at Susan. In a way, she irritated him. How in the world did this woman, whom he didn't know, suddenly get plopped down into the middle of their special days of being together as family? What was worse, Jim couldn't get her eyes out of his mind, and he couldn't help but notice how beautiful she was. *Whoa! Whoa, Jim ol' boy!* he said to himself. *You heard her say she was angry at God. She's not the type of lady who would make a preacher's wife!* Jim quickly stopped his thought process and adjusted the rearview mirror to look at himself. *Where did that come from?* he wondered.

The cargo area of the Jeep was stacked full of hunting supplies, so Jim had to rely on the side mirrors to keep an eye on traffic. With the rearview mirror now at his disposal, Jim discreetly moved it a quarter of an inch so that he could again look at Susan. She and Andrea continued to talk and chuckle between themselves.

Jim forced his mind to think on safer things: his church and his congregation. He was only an assistant pastor, yet he carried a burden for his people. He knew there would be fireworks and some opposition when the time came for the congregation to welcome an ex-convict into their midst. He reflected back to a couple of hours earlier when no less than three different families—none too quietly or discreetly—had mentioned that they might have to look for another church if such a person were allowed to fellowship and be present among them and their family.

Jim's mind floated to Scripture about forgiveness—that if you don't forgive, you can't be forgiven. It was one of the basic truths of Christianity, yet it was such a test for so many people. Jim's heart ached. This would certainly be an issue that he and the congregation would have to deal with in the near future.

Jim looked down at his cell phone sitting in the empty cup holder. Pastor Burns was coming home this afternoon, and Jim knew that he needed to brace him for the calls he would most likely be receiving in response to the sermon he had preached that morning. Jim took the cell phone and punched in his pastor's number. He was still in Virginia, so he could legally talk and drive. He took another peek in the mirror to take a quick glance at Susan's eyes. When he saw that they were closed, a hesitant disappointment hit him. He shook himself and listened to the phone ring.

"Hello?" said a voice as Pastor Burns answered the phone.

Jim talked pleasantries with the pastor for a minute and then touched on his sermon and the reactions he had received from some of the congregation. Pastor Burns sighed and acknowledged that the people in the congregation were at different stages of growth. Some were mature, and some were still babes in Christ, but they were all brothers and sisters. "Thanks for the heads-up, Jim," he said. "I'll be sensitive. We'll need to get the church council, the pastors' council and the deacons together. We will need a plan to ensure that our church is a safe haven and not a country club."

Jim thanked Pastor Burns and hung up. Again, he looked into the rearview mirror to glance at Susan. "Anybody need to make a pit stop?" he asked.

"Yes, I do," both women answered together from the back of the Jeep.

Jim looked at the signs along the road. "We have a Hardees or Burger King coming up. We can pull off in one mile." The ladies scrunched around in the back seat as they started preparing themselves for the brief stop.

To George, Jim was the best cousin-in-law a man could have. The hobbies they shared and the things they enjoyed doing together made them like brothers—even closer than brothers. Their hearts beat as one. George loved Jim for who he was, and Jim's favorite first cousin, Andrea, was the love of his life. Andrea was as kind and tender and sweet as any woman George had ever met. When he had first met Andrea, he couldn't take his eyes off of her. He had been struck by her beauty and charm. In addition to her natural beauty, she had a beauty that came from within.

George was perceptive—he hadn't become successful in business by not being sharp or knowing how to deal with people—and as he sat in the shotgun seat of the Jeep, chattering and bantering back and forth with Jim, he was laughing inside. Watching Jim and his mannerisms made him think back three or four years ago when he had first met Andrea. George knew that Jim would deny having any feelings for Susan if he kidded him about it, so he just watched Jim continue to adjust his mirror and sneak quick peeks at the women in the back. *These next several days are going to be dynamite,* George thought. *A lot of hunting will be going on – and not just deer hunting!*

George laughed as he sat up and stretched as much as he could in the Jeep. Jim looked over at him. "What's so funny?" he asked.

"You," George said.

"Me?" Jim said. "There's nothing funny about me! I'm just excited to be going on this vacation. These are some of my favorite days of the year."

"A lot of hunting going on," George said. Jim threw George a sideways glance as he parked the Jeep Cherokee.

"That's right, George," he said. "A lot of hunting. I have a buck to kill, and I think I know where he'll be."

"Right," George replied. "A whole lot of huntin' goin' on."

The women looked at the men as they climbed out of the back of the Jeep and headed for Hardees. Jim felt his neck get a little warm and pulled George aside. "Look, George," he said, "I'm not up here for that kind of hunting. I'm up here to hunt deer."

"Right, Jim," George answered. "Happy hunting, buddy. Happy hunting."

Jim threw up his hands in disgust and walked into Hardees. Two hours down, two hours to go. He looked forward to the vegetable soup with the big chunks of deer roast in it that he would soon be eating. It would taste so good on this cool evening. The warm wood stove, the bantering that would follow, maybe a hunting video, all the talk, all the bragging, all the stories. Jim shook himself and pinched his arm to make sure he wasn't dreaming. He wasn't dreaming. It was that time of year again.

As Jim stood in line to buy his drink, George and the two women came up and stood behind him. Jim was acutely aware of Susan standing there and the remarks that George had made. George was always teasing him about finding the right girl. He often reminded Jim that he was twenty-seven years old and that time was slipping away. *She's not my type,*

Jim said to himself, again wondering why he was thinking about this so much.

Jim ordered his drink, paid for it and stood to the side. Susan, feeling the friction of her actions, asked, "You're not buying my drink, Jim?"

Jim looked around, flustered. "Well, I didn't know . . . I . . . well, yes if you need me to buy you a drink . . . I'll be happy to buy you a drink, Susan."

"That's okay, Jim," she said. "I'll get my own. I just wondered if you would."

Jim looked at Susan again. Her eyes mesmerized him. He could look so deep into those eyes—those eyes with twenty different shades of brown.

Susan laughed. "Do you like my eyes, Jim?"

"Huh?" Jim asked. "Well . . . they are," he stammered, "they are pretty."

Susan laughed again. "Well, I have what the good Lord gave me. At least He gave me these eyes—He's taken so much else away."

Jim took his cup without saying a word and went and got his drink. He couldn't understand her. She must be one hurting, confused person to accuse God of taking her husband. His heart ached for her.

After the others had paid for their drinks, they all walked slowly back to the Jeep. "It looks as though it will be a beautiful day to hunt tomorrow," George said.

"Yep, let's see," Jim said. "One, two, three. Sam, you and me. Sounds like three deer on the meat pole."

George laughed. "That's a little optimistic, but it could happen."

Sam and George had roomed together the last few years of college. That friendship had proved to be a blessing in many ways. Not only had George found a life-long hunting buddy in Sam, but the friendship had opened the door for Sam and Jim to become acquainted. Now, all three had a wonderful place to hunt together at Sam and Martha's cabin.

Pennsylvania was as good a place as any to enjoy the quiet and solitude provided by a comfortable mountain cabin. In fact, George and Jim couldn't have asked for a better location. Pennsylvania had a lot of deer, and most of the bucks that were killed each year were bagged on opening day because the hunting pressure was so heavy. However, George and Jim were blessed by the fact that Sam had 300 acres of private wooded land on his farm. It was the perfect place to hunt because it wasn't near the hunting pressure, and Sam was able to make sure that there was plenty of feed for the deer year-round. It was a hunting paradise.

Jim grinned. "Well, the only thing I'm going to say is that you all can wait until Tuesday or Wednesday, but I have every intention of killing my buck tomorrow morning."

George laughed. "Yeah, and then you'll keep on hunting, right?"

Jim gave George another sideways glance and then decided to ignore him. The group piled into the Jeep and were soon on their way again.

Chapter 3

As Jim started up the road, Andrea, in the back seat, was looking out the window. Her mind was floating as she sipped her Dr. Pepper. *Three deer on the meat pole tomorrow? Ha, ha! Maybe there will be four! But the men wouldn't know that. Or maybe there will only be one – maybe it will be mine*! She grinned for a moment at the thought and then frowned. Would she get to hunt now that she was Susan-sitting? How would Susan handle it? What would Susan think?

Andrea knew that Susan had issues that needed to be dealt with and that she would have to spend time with her to help her work through those issues. Susan had been raised in the city and wasn't accustomed to the country and hunting lifestyle. It was different. It was new to her. Would she be able to settle down and relax during the next several days? Andrea sure did hope so.

Andrea continued to sip her Dr Pepper and look out the window, her mind in a state of oblivion, daydreaming about slipping out to that little funnel she had found. She had never field dressed a deer by herself, though she had watched it done many times. It wasn't that she was afraid of blood and intestines—she felt that she could field dress the deer without any trouble—but she was concerned about how she would get the deer back to the meat pole and hang it up. Yet God had helped her think of a way to get the rifle into the jeep without the men knowing, and God would provide for this, too. She sat there with a smile on her face, thankful that God led the smallest details of her life.

Susan sipped her drink and watched Andrea's facial expressions. Andrea was lost in a world of her own, and Susan wished she knew what it was. A feeling of jealously swept over her. Andrea had her career and a living husband who loved and adored her. She and George seemed to enjoy spending time together. Susan sighed, hurting for what she had lost. She and her husband had been close, and the pain and anguish she had experienced when he was killed were beyond words.

Her eyes flickered to Jim's profile in the front seat. She had noticed earlier that he didn't have a ring on his left hand, and she wondered if he was married. *That's an odd thought,* she said to herself. *He's a minister, for crying out loud!* Still, his black hair, his black eyes and the way he carried himself—she couldn't quit looking at him and wondering what type of guy he was. If he was a minister, then he must have certain qualities about him that would speak well for him.

Susan thought about the pain and the anguish she had been through. She had tried counseling, but the counselors had said that it was time to move on, that it was time to live again. Instead, Susan clung to her memories and to the pain. She tried not to blame herself for her husband's death, but she couldn't stop wondering why she hadn't been with him that fateful day and how God could be so unjust as to take somebody so young who was so loved.

Susan looked again at Jim and noticed that his ear was red. She wondered if this was from embarrassment or if she was imagining things. She had heard George's teasing, and she now realized that Jim had to be aware she was in the back seat. A part of her giggled inside as she thought of the uneasiness that she was creating in him. She wondered why she had asked him if he would buy her a drink. She certainly had plenty of money in her pocket. Between her husband's life insurance, the car insurance from the accident and the inheritance she had received from her late parents, finances were definitely not a problem. Had she subconsciously stepped in with George to embarrass Jim and make somebody else feel pain? She suddenly realized that she had been pretty naïve in coming unannounced for a visit to Andrea and George's. Yet did God move in ways beyond her, even though she had doubts and was angry at Him.

As she thought about Jim, she began to realize that she wanted very much to be a part of the next several days. It would be a totally new experience for her—dressing in a completely different way for the outdoors and being in a rustic environment where it was dark when the lights went out because the city lights weren't shining. She wondered what it was that made these men tick and gave them the enthusiasm and excitement for what they were going to do.

Susan sipped on her Dr Pepper and again looked at Andrea. Andrea glanced back at her with a grin in her eyes, gave her the thumbs up sign, and quietly mouthed the words, "We have a secret."

Susan smiled and looked out the window. They were just driving into Pennsylvania, and suddenly she saw some deer in the field. She squealed, and at the same time George yelled, "Look! There are some deer!"

"Susan, you're doing good," Andrea said. "You're seeing deer already. You're seeing them as fast as the men are. You're going to have fun."

"I don't know how I saw them," Susan said. "It's just that suddenly they were there."

George laughed. "That's the way deer are—suddenly they are just there."

Jim spoke up. "George, you know that's not always the way it is. You can help yourself spot deer."

"I see my share," George replied.

"Yes, but for those women back there, we need to explain how you see deer."

"Oh, right," George said. "These ladies—these poor, helpless ladies who need to be taught how to see deer!"

"We're not helpless!" Andrea and Susan said at the same time. "And Susan saw the deer as fast as anyone," Andrea added.

"Okay, okay!" Jim said. "But if you want to see deer, you have to look for horizontal lines. In the woods, nearly everything is vertical. Deer are brown and naturally camouflaged, so if you look for movement and horizontal lines, you'll see them a lot faster."

Andrea thought about that for a moment and realized that Jim was right, but she didn't let on. Instead, she looked at Susan and again mouthed the words, "We've got a secret." Then she looked up to the front seat and said, "We're not as helpless and hopeless as you think. We'll do our share in making these next several days successful."

George and Jim both grinned at each other. George glanced back at the two women and said, "Yes, you can help us be successful. We men can cook, but your cooking is much better. You keep food on the table for us, and we'll be successful. Sandwiches in our lunch, hot meals, morning and evening . . ."

Andrea rolled her eyes. Oh, how she wanted to hang a deer on that meat pole. She looked at Susan and winked.

Chapter 4

It was a little after 5:30 that evening when the group pulled into the lane to the cabin. When Susan saw the structure, she wondered, *Do people really live in that thing?* The exterior siding was weather-beaten, and a patch of shingles was missing on one corner of the roof, leaving several rafters exposed in the two-foot overhang of the eaves.

When the Jeep came to a stop, Jim and George opened their doors and jumped out, stretched and let out a war whoop. They had arrived. Andrea and Susan looked at each other, rolled their eyes, opened their own doors and crawled out.

Just then, Sam came to the door, threw out his hands and said, "All right, boys! This is it! Here we are again!" George and Jim both started dancing a small jig. Susan wondered how grown men could act so much like kids over the prospects of harvesting a poor deer.

"Susan, quick," Andrea whispered, "help me get your sleeping bag into the cabin."

The women opened the back of the Jeep, got the sleeping bag out and carried it inside. "This is the bedroom that George and I always stay in," Andrea whispered. "There are numerous guns setting along the back wall, and I think I can set my gun up among them and no one will even notice that it's there." She slid the gun carefully out from the sleeping bag and set it in the rack. They looked at each other and grinned. Andrea felt as though she had pulled off one part of her plan.

Andrea and Susan walked back out into the main room of the cabin. "Sure does smell good in here," Andrea said.

Susan wrinkled her nose, took a big whiff and agreed. "Mercy, I didn't realize how hungry I was!" she said.

The women headed for the stove, slipped the lid off the big kettle and peeked inside. The kettle was full of vegetable venison soup.

"Sure does smell good," Andrea said. "I'm about to starve."

The women walked back into the living room and looked out the front door. Sam, George and Jim were just beginning to unload the Cherokee. They could hear the men begin to banter about who would get his deer first.

"I know where there's a big one," Sam said. "I've been watching him all summer long. I have him figured out, and I believe he'll be mine in the morning."

Jim laughed. "I know the spot where I'm going. It has produced a nice deer year after year. If a big ol' buck comes through that draw, he'll be mine!"

George looked at them and laughed. "Y'all are so hung up on shooting the biggest deer. I'd rather just find a legal buck that I can shoot so I can have more tender meat for eating. And since you have to pay extra for doe tags, how many doe tags did you get, Jim?"

"Only one," Jim said.

"Me, too," said George.

Sam looked at them and smiled. "I have two. Oh, we'll do okay these next couple of days, guys."

As the men unloaded the Jeep, they noticed a beautiful sunset showering out red streaks across the sky. "Red sky in the morning, shepherds take warning," George said. "Red sky at night, shepherds delight." Tomorrow would be a delight indeed.

"It will be perfect in the morning," Jim said.

"Yes, it will," George agreed.

"Right now, though, let's get this stuff in," Jim said. "I'm about to starve."

The women came out and started picking up suitcases, gun cases and other items to help get everything into the cabin.

"Sam, where's Martha?" Andrea asked.

"She went back to our house for a little bit," Sam replied. "She was here earlier and helped me with the soup. She'll be back soon."

"That's good," Andrea said. "That way we can eat."

George and Andrea walked into the cabin and carried their bags into their bedroom. When Jim walked in, he scratched his head and pondered his next move. Sam and Martha had their bedroom, and Andrea and George had theirs. They used the same ones year after year. Jim started to take his things to his room, but then stopped. He had a dilemma. What was he going to do?

George looked up at him. "So, where are you hanging out, Jim? Where are you going to put all of your stuff?"

Andrea and Susan overheard the conversation. "I'll sleep on the couch," Susan said. "I'm the odd man out."

"No, no way!" Jim said. "I'll sleep on the couch. You put your things in the bedroom. My things can go here in the corner. I'll be okay. I'll sleep on the couch."

Jim said it in a way that made Susan feel like she shouldn't argue. She looked at Jim, smiled and said, "Thanks. I appreciate the fact that you're taking it in stride that I interrupted your party and the way you normally do things."

"Don't worry about it," Jim said. "We'll be fine."

Andrea glanced at Susan, and Susan glanced back at Andrea.

"Come on, Susan," Andrea said. "Let's get your things into your bedroom." Jim threw his duffle bag and sleeping bag into the corner, turned around, stretched again and let out a war whoop. He was here again—to spend the evening together as a group, to get up in the morning and go hunting with the guys . . . life was good.

Suddenly, he stopped as he remembered the church service that morning and the families who had been so distraught. A slight frown spread across his face. "God," he quietly prayed, "be with the families who are hurting and frustrated this evening. They feel like their world is being threatened. I'm on an emotional high, and they're on an emotional low. Give them peace. Give them the desire to search Your Word and seek Your face."

Jim ended his prayer and looked up. "Okay, ladies," he said. "What's for supper?" He knew full well what the meal would be. It was a tradition, like the whole hunting camp and the whole hunting week that they had spent together each fall for the past four or five years. "It sure does smell good. I believe I could eat a gallon!"

George laughed. "I hope not, because by the time I eat my gallon and these women eat their half gallon, there won't be enough left for you to eat that much."

Jim patted his stomach and rolled his eyes. "I'm ready to give it a good try."

Just then, they heard a car pull up in the driveway, the gravel crunching in the lane. "That's Martha," said Sam. "That's good. Now we can eat."

Andrea and Susan quickly went to set the table. As Andrea began to set the six plates and bowls, she smiled to herself and thought, *I'm going to sit with my man George, and Sam and Martha are going to sit together, so, like it or not, Susan and Jim are going to have to sit together.* A grin spread across Andrea's face. Susan had a look of slight horror on her face as she realized the awkwardness that soon would be thrust upon her.

When Martha came into the cabin, Andrea called to her and said, "Let me introduce you to Susan, a friend of mine. We went through nurses' training in college together. She arrived at noon today for a visit, so we brought her along."

Martha smiled. "It's good to have you here, Susan. Make yourself at home. Just don't eat all of the soup, because we're hungry!"

Susan glanced at the pot of soup on the stove and laughed. If these six people ate all that soup, they would burst!

"Looks as though you're ready for us to sit down," Martha said. "Thanks Andrea and Susan, for setting the table. Go ahead and ladle up the soup into the bowls and pour the drink. We have the crackers."

Andrea brought out a plate filled with celery, carrots and broccoli with a dip in the middle. "I thought I would bring this to give us something to nibble on besides the soup," she said. She set it down in the middle of the table.

"Time to eat," Martha said.

Susan hung back at the stove, not sure where she was supposed to sit. She didn't want to interfere, and she didn't want to run ahead of the group. Martha and Sam took the places where they always sat, and George and Andrea took their normal spots as well. Jim looked at the last two spots.

"May I sit next to you, Jim?" Susan asked timidly. "It looks as if the rest of the places are taken."

"No problem," Jim said. "We all need a place to sit and eat, and that there seat is as good as any place else."

They sat down, and everyone except Susan automatically reached out to hold hands around the table. However, she quickly realized what was going on and reached for the hands that had been extended toward her; Jim's on one side, Andrea's on the other.

"Whose turn is it to pray?" George asked.

"I don't know whose turn it is, but I'll be happy to pray," Jim said. "I'm about to starve."

When Jim started to pray, he had a hitch in his voice. He was holding Susan's hand, and it felt a little damp, yet so soft. A slight shiver went through him as he concentrated on trying to pray, thanking God for a safe trip, for the time of the year, and for the food. When the prayer was over, he let go of Susan's hand, and as he did so he glanced up and saw that she was looking at him. She quickly dropped her eyelashes. At that moment, something stirred within Jim, and he wanted to look into those brown eyes. The different shades of brown continued to captivate him. The electricity that had gone through his hand when he held Susan's was something he had never felt before.

Everyone started eating the soup. The group began talking and jesting with each other, with three conversations going at once. It seemed as though everyone was talking at once and no one was listening. Susan sat quietly as she listened to the chattering around her, feeling the closeness of the group. This was all so new for her. She wondered about Jim. When she took his big, strong hand, she could sense the shudder that went through him. She snuck a quick peek at him and admired his facial features and his easygoing manner, and as she did so she thought of her deceased husband. The two men were so different. She had been in love with her husband, and he had been a good man, but she couldn't remember feeling the same electric shock when she had held hands with him as she had felt when Jim held her hand to pray.

"You're awfully quiet, Susan," Andrea said.

"I'm just taking it all in," Susan said. "All of your light-hearted teasing; all of your chit-chat. I'm trying to figure out how you all can eat and talk at the same time."

George got up from the table. His bowl was already empty. "I'm getting seconds," he said. "Anybody else need any more? Give me your bowls."

Sam and Jim handed him their bowls. They both were about empty. George ladled the soup again, came back from the stove and handed each of the men their bowls. "You gals better hurry up and eat," he said to Andrea, Susan and Martha. "You ladies are slow eaters. We men will eat it all out from underneath you!"

"You better save us some," warned Martha. "We might be slow, but we have healthy appetites. And we have a lot to do over these next several days that will require plenty of adequate nourishment."

"Humph!" Jim grunted. "Y'all have a lot to do. We're the ones who are going to be out there hunting."

"Aw, that's right," teased Martha. "You have to go out and sit down in the woods and do nothing all day long. Just sit."

"That's hard work," Sam told her. "It takes a lot of work to sit there. You're under a mental strain, listening, looking, looking, listening . . ."

"Oh, I'm sure you're under a lot of strain," Martha said. "Well, if you're under such strain, why do you do it?"

George grinned. "It's the best strain I've been under all year!"

Martha shook her head. Sometimes she couldn't fathom the deep-seated drive that sent these men out early, before daylight each morning, with all their hunting toys and all they had to accumulate, just to go sit in the woods.

George grinned. "Well, we have to be energetic enough to get to where we want to be, and then we have to be lazy enough to sit and stay there," he said. "Yet we still need to expend our energy in listening and watching and being attentive to the woods around us, so we need to eat. I'm wondering about that third bowl of soup."

"Not before we get seconds," Andrea piped up. She got up and went over to the stove. "Still plenty of soup here. Do you need some more, Susan, Martha?"

"Half a bowl," Susan said. "I'm not anticipating working that hard tomorrow. And I'm getting full."

Martha laughed. "I'll take another full bowl. It's pretty good soup, even though Sam and I did make it."

George and Jim worked on their third bowl. The chit-chat continued across and around the room. Susan was quiet as she ate her soup, wondering where the men put it all. She was feeling overwhelmed by the atmosphere and the excitement of the people who were in the room with her.

Jim reared back on his chair and patted his stomach. "There is one question I have about tomorrow morning," he said.

"Oh, no!" Andrea exclaimed. "I thought you were all prepared and ready. I thought you knew what you were going to do. I thought you knew where your buck was."

"Oh, yeah, yeah," Jim said. "That's not my question. That's not my problem."

All eyes turned to Jim.

"I'm just wondering what's for breakfast and who's fixing it," he said. "You can't go to the woods on an empty stomach."

Martha and Andrea both threw their napkins at Jim and laughed.

"You know good and well who's fixing breakfast in the morning," Andrea said, "and you know what it will be."

Jim looked at her innocently, his eyes big. "Who? What?"

"You're the one who fixes breakfast on Monday morning."

"Well, how many of you like leftover soup in the morning?"

Groans went around the table. Of course, they all knew what was for breakfast, and they knew that it would be early. On Monday morning, Jim always made fried sausage and pancakes with lots of syrup—something that would stick with a man.

Susan pushed back her chair. "Can I help you, Andrea? Martha, can I help you wash the dishes? I'd be glad to wash if you tell me where things are and what to do."

"No, you certainly may not," Andrea and Martha said.

Susan started to protest, but Andrea interrupted her. "You can't help us because we're not the ones doing it," she explained. "The men have to wash the dishes. We ladies are going over there to the couch to sit down and relax and watch a video. We're not up here to work the whole time. These men have to do something."

Susan again marveled at the camaraderie and the spirit that encircled the five friends. A sigh slipped from her lips as she wondered what it would be like to have this kind of close-knit friendship on a regular basis. She had spent less than a day with these people, and already something was stirring within her. She was beginning to feel alive again.

Chapter 5

The men worked as a team, cleaning the table, drawing dishwater, and washing and drying the dishes. In a matter of what seemed like minutes, the job was done and the extra soup had been put in a bowl and into the fridge. The women put a video into the VCR. The men groaned. Of all things they could have watched, they had chosen *Charlotte's Web*.

"Hey, Andrea," George said. "You missed the hunting videos."

"Oh, we missed them all right," Andrea said. "We missed them all around to find *Charlotte's Web*."

The men groaned again.

Jim looked at Susan and caught her looking at him. Something about that woman set him on edge. He had never experienced the feeling of frustration and nervousness that she was bringing out of him. *Is that what love is?* Jim thought. He again wondered where those thoughts were coming from. Susan had her problems. She hadn't been very conscientious in her planning by showing up at George and Andrea's the way she did. Jim wondered what kind of wife she would be. He flicked the dishtowel onto the counter in frustration with himself for letting his thoughts again wander. Yet, somehow, he couldn't get her out of his mind.

Susan continued to discreetly watch Jim, a curl on her lips. She realized the effect that she was having on him. She asked herself if this was a road that she wanted to travel. Her thoughts went back to her deceased husband, to the tortures and agonies of these past two years of trying to adjust, to accept and to learn to live again. She pictured herself beside Jim and shook her head. He was a pastor, and she certainly could not see herself as a minister's wife.

Get a hold of yourself, Susan! she said to herself. *This will all be over in a couple of days. I'll spend some time with Andrea, and then I'll be on my way back home to more long faces, more lonely nights, more trying to live each day as a walking shell of frustration.* She thought of the last half of the day and realized that she had enjoyed it far more than she ever would have dared to hope.

Jim picked up a deck of Rook cards from the kitchen counter. "Who all wants to play Rook?" he asked. "It sure beats watching *Charlotte's Web.*

There was a murmur of consent among the men.

"Will we have four or six players?" Jim said.

"I'd rather not play," said Martha. "I'll be content to sit and listen to you all and to *Charlotte's Web.*"

"Rook?" Susan asked. "What kind of game is that?"

"Oh, come now," said Andrea. "You've never played Rook?"

"I've played many card games, but never Rook. What is it like?"

Andrea looked at George, Jim and Sam. "We four can play, and I'll help Susan learn by watching me."

The men agreed, pulled chairs up to the table and sat around it. Susan sat beside Andrea with Jim to her right and the other couple sitting around them. They played Rook for an hour and a half.

Andrea was the first to reach a score of 1,000 points. "We won!" she said. "Shows who can play Rook."

"That's right," Susan agreed. "We can play Rook. We showed them."

Jim looked at Susan and raised his eyebrows. "Right . . . you said you didn't know how to play, and yet, you beat us."

Susan grinned. "Well, I did give Andrea moral support, against all of you men."

Jim chuckled, tossed the cards on the table and stood up. "Well, tomorrow's a big day, fellows," he said. "I think it's about time to turn in. I want to get up early in the morning, and I need to get some sleep. So . . . if you all wouldn't mind getting out of my bedroom, I will officially retire for the evening."

George laughed. "We're in your bedroom, all right. That couch will do you good for tonight. It's plenty long enough."

Jim looked up at the TV screen where *Charlotte's Web* was playing. The video was almost over. He would be glad to throw his sleeping bag down on the sofa and lie on top of it. He didn't really need to be inside of it—the wood stove made it very warm in the cabin.

The one bathroom in the cabin was off to the side of the three doors that led to the bedrooms. Jim went to the bathroom, brushed his teeth, and got ready for bed. He put on his white thermal underwear, which kept him warm while he was out hunting, as his pajamas. It covered him well enough that it didn't bother him to parade around in them in front of the others. Sam and Martha went to their bedroom, and George and Andrea went to theirs.

Susan walked to her bedroom, turned and again looked at Jim. "I'm sorry I put you out of your bedroom," she said.

Jim waved his hands. "Don't think twice about it. I'm fine on the couch. It will soon be morning, and we'll be hunting."

After everyone had gone to bed, Jim lay on the couch, his mind working over the events of the day. He again prayed for the congregation back home. What would it take to heal the hurts, anguish and anger in the church? How could he help those within the congregation understand that forgiveness was not only important but also essential in the Christian life? Yes, steps would have to be taken to dispel the fears of the people. The church would even have to take steps to ensure his "freed" friend that someone wouldn't try to set him up on false charges to get him sent back to prison and out of their company.

After Jim prayed for his congregation, he prayed for the safety of himself and his friends for the hunt that would start in the morning. As he prayed, a vivid picture of Susan suddenly came into his mind. He frowned. Why was he continuing to think about her? There was something about her that irritated him, but also something about her that drew him. He kept on wanting to look at her and her eyes—eyes that seemed to swallow up his whole being when he stared into them. The night wore on, and he fell asleep.

Susan laid her head back on her pillow and stared toward the ceiling. For once, she wasn't feeling the anxiety, frustration and strangling closeness of life. There was a small sense of excitement in her inner being. She marveled at what she had experienced the past twelve hours, wondering how her life could change so much in such a short period of time and who had changed it. Immediately, the face of Jim crossed her mind, and she wondered what it would be like to have him as a friend and to have him hold her. How she missed the loving touch of a husband; a man who would whisper sweet nothings to her, breathe heavily on the back of her neck and nibble on her ear. Susan shook herself. *Get real!* she said to herself.

Susan lay there, looking up at the ceiling. "God," she breathed, "these last two years have been a nightmare. I haven't been able to cope. I've blamed You for so much, yet,

I know that You're a God of love. God, please help me to continue to enjoy these next several days. Show me the paths that You want me to travel."

A peace instantly came over Susan that she hadn't felt since her husband had died. With a contented sigh, she snuggled into her sleeping bag and soon drifted off to sleep.

George looked at Andrea and smiled. "Be nice, George," Andrea whispered. "I can already see in your eyes what you're thinking."

"What I'm thinking?" George responded. "I don't have to think. It's clear as day. They keep looking at each other. It's too obvious not to notice. Good ol' buddy Jim will get some good ribbing out of this. I'll enjoy seeing him squirm."

"Be nice, George," Andrea said again. "Yes, you're right. I've seen how they look at each other. I saw Jim jump when he held Susan's hand during prayer at supper. But just lie low and let things progress. Let's just wait and see what happens."

George pulled Andrea close to him and gave her a kiss. "All right," he murmured, "have it your way. I've got to get some sleep. I'm going hunting in the morning."

And they slept.

Jim suddenly awoke. The wood stove was still pouring out heat, and he lay there on top of his sleeping bag without any covers. His white thermal long johns had been more than adequate; he had worn them more to cover himself than for warmth. He looked at his watch. It was 3:30 in the morning. He would have to get up in an hour and a half to fix breakfast, but right now he had to get up to go to the bathroom. He remembered where the furniture was and carefully made his way through the cabin without turning on the lights.

Susan awoke in her bedroom. She normally slept through the night, but with all the tea that she had drunk the evening before, she found herself needing to go to the bathroom. She didn't want to create any commotion or wake anyone up, so she crawled out of bed and quietly began sneaking toward the bathroom. When she was outside of her bedroom door, she remembered Jim sleeping on the couch. She had her nightgown on, but she thought that she could surely sneak into the bathroom and back to her room without being seen. She tried to remember exactly where the bathroom was from her bedroom, and carefully made her way in that direction.

Just as she got to the bathroom, Jim opened the door from the inside and walked headlong into her. "Umph," Susan said, stifling a cry of surprise and pain. Her eye had caught Jim's cheekbone. Jim stumbled and let out a "woof" as he grabbed Susan to keep from falling.

"What in the world!" he said. "Who, what? What's going on?"

"Umph!" Susan cried out this time. She was mortified, and her cheek hurt. She had to get to the bathroom. "Who is this?" she squealed.

"Guess," was all that Jim could say.

"Jim, I'm so, so sorry. I didn't see you."

"No, and I didn't see you either."

"We're supposed to be quiet. We're not supposed to wake anybody up. I need to go to the bathroom, Jim."

"Well, I don't need to go now, I've just been," Jim laughed. He touched his cheek. "Ouch!" he said. "That hurts."

"I . . . ah . . . oh, I'm so sorry," Susan mumbled. She ducked into the bathroom and quickly closed the door.

Jim shook his head in pain and touched his cheek again. "Ouch!" he said, again. He could feel that it was already starting to turn puffy. *That's all I need,* he thought. *Why in the world did that woman have to come along with us on the hunting trip?* At the same time, Jim remembered holding on to her arms and the smell of her perfume as she stood in front of him. Mixed emotions swept over him. He carefully made his way back to the couch and lay down, his mind in a whirl. He lay there for a while, staring at the ceiling and touching his cheek again. Oh, it smarted. He knew that he should put ice on it, but he didn't feel like getting up again—and with Susan still in the bathroom, he certainly wasn't about to get up again.

Jim heard the bathroom door ease open. "May I come out now?" Susan squeaked. "Clear the way; I'm coming through."

Jim grunted.

Susan quickly tiptoed to her bedroom door, shut it and lay back down. She put her fingers to her eye. Wow, it hurt. How in the world did that happen? She had tried to be so careful and had ended up running right smack into Jim. How embarrassing!

She lay there in the dark and touched her face again, realizing that her eye was starting to swell. She knew that she should put some ice on it, but she wasn't about to go back out to the kitchen. She was horrified as she thought about what had happened. Yet at the same time, she remembered Jim's hands around her arms, holding her, the closeness of him, his breath on her face as he exhaled from the bump. Deep within her, a longing began to build as she remembered what it was like to have a man hold her close.

Susan's emotions tumbled over themselves in her mind, like water over Niagara Falls, roaring at her. After her talk with God a few hours earlier when she was settling down for the night, she realized that the idea of Jim being a preacher didn't sound nearly so bad any more. She wondered what he was really like. Why was she having these feelings, these attractions? Should she let herself feel anything? Was she being disloyal to her deceased husband? How long should she grieve before moving on?

Susan turned and tossed. Sleep wouldn't come. Her mind kept cranking and winding like a yo-yo, going up and down and in circles. She kept thinking and pondering and wondering. It had been years since she'd had this much fun or been so carefree. She had actually flirted a little by the way she lowered her eyelashes. What was she doing here in Pennsylvania, in a hunting cabin of all places?

Slowly, the yo-yo of emotions subsided, and Susan slept.

Chapter 6

Jim's alarm rang at five o'clock. The morning had arrived. He piled out of bed, off the sofa, and quickly remembered his cheek. "Oooh," he said, putting his hand to the side of his face. It hurt. He knocked lightly on Sam and George's doors and went about preparing breakfast: sausages, pancakes and orange juice. He would also fix himself a sandwich to eat at ten in the morning. He would come back for lunch, but a little food on the deer stand certainly couldn't hurt.

The smell of breakfast compelled George and Sam to get out of bed. Their wives turned over; they didn't have to get up, so they went back to sleep. Jim was putting the sausages and pancakes on the plates when George came out of the bathroom.

"You in a hurry, Jim?" he asked.

"Well, we need to get out there before daylight and be ready to go," Jim said.

"I'm talking about the camouflage paint on your cheekbone."

"I didn't put any camouflage paint . . ." Jim suddenly stopped. He raised his hand, again, to his cheek. Ouch!

"That's not camouflage paint?" George asked smugly. "Well, it wasn't there last night. Let me take a look at that, Jim."

"Eat your breakfast," Jim retorted.

"What is this, Jim? It looks like you've been struck by a bear."

"It's nothing."

"Darkest, puffiest nothing I've ever seen," George said. "Hey Sam, look-y here. Jim got swatted by a big mosquito in the middle of the night."

"Eat your breakfast," Jim growled.

Sam came over and looked at Jim. "Pretty bad mosquito bite, if you ask me, to cause that kind of anguish."

Jim stared at Sam and snorted. "I said, eat your breakfast!"

"Who got you, Jim?" Sam asked. "What's going on? You're supposed to sleep at night."

"I did sleep last night," Jim said. "Eat your breakfast."

"Well, looks like we need to find out how the other person looks, or the door or the wall . . . what'd you do, Jim?"

"Eat your breakfast, guys!"

"Now, don't get touchy with us," said Sam. "Who'd you hit?"

"I just went to the bathroom. Something got in my way."

George looked at Sam. "Umm-hmm. Sam, did you hear anything last night?"

"Nope," said Sam. "I was sleeping."

"I didn't hear anything either," George said. "It looks like Jim, though, was prowling around last night. He's liable to go to sleep on his deer stand this morning. I bet you he won't kill any deer today. He'll be sleeping."

Jim looked at them and grinned. "I'll show you," he said.

The fellows ate their breakfast, climbed into Sam's truck and made their way to the stands where they wanted to hunt. Sam dropped George off first. "Happy hunting, buddy," he said. "Get a big one."

George grinned, flashed a thumbs up, turned his flashlight on and headed toward the tree he wanted to climb. He had been waiting all summer long to try out his new self-climbing tree stand. He would be up that tree in no time!

Sam drove another half mile and dropped off Jim. "Happy hunting, big boy," he said. "Stay awake."

Jim looked at Sam. "Happy hunting to you, too, fella," he growled. "Don't shoot that big one until he comes by me. I'll show you all who's awake."

Sam smiled and drove on to his own stand.

Darkness fought to keep its hold on the forest, but, minute by minute, it grew lighter. First, Jim could see his hand in front of his face, and then the rifle in his hand. Finally, he could make out the ground and start to see the leaves. He put his fingers to his cheekbone. He could tell that it was still puffy. He knew it was sore. He wondered what Susan looked like. Why in the world did she have to choose that precise moment to have to go to the bathroom?

Jim sat there and closed his eyes, waiting for the darkness to give up and, like a great cloak, gradually be lifted and thrown off. Light began to penetrate the woods more and more. Finally, Jim said to himself, *"I believe I can see enough. It's light enough. The season has begun."*

He looked at his watch. Another three minutes and hunting season would officially begin in the state of Pennsylvania. He settled into his summit tree stand. Oh, the pleasures of opening morning in Pennsylvania. Already he heard one or two shots in the distance—shots on other farms where somebody was having early morning success. He had both a buck tag and a doe tag, but today he would concentrate on a buck. There would be plenty of time to shoot a doe, but now was the time to get his Pennsylvania buck.

He sat there motionless. His eyes slowly traveled from the edge of the laurel thicket, through the small draw where heavy trails crisscrossed the saddle below him. Before the morning was over, he was sure that he would see deer. Jim was relaxed and content, his ears on sharp alert, listening for any little twig that might break. His eyes continued to scan back and forth for any detection of movement.

Slowly, he raised his hand to his face. His cheekbone sure was painful. He again wondered about Susan and what her face must look like. He had certainly been surprised when they had slammed into each other. They had hit solidly. He had actually seen stars.

As Jim thought of Susan, he let his mind wander back to the events of the previous day. After the church service, he had sat in his office and prayed for God to help him find his mate, someone whom he could love and cherish and with whom he could have children. He wanted to teach his sons—and maybe even his daughters—how to hunt, enjoy the outdoors and live life to the fullest. And he wanted to do it with his wife, his best friend, at his side. Was Susan that woman?

Jim slowly shook his head. He certainly doubted it. But, somehow, she created a disturbance within his mind. And those eyes—those multi-colored brown eyes that he could just keep looking into further and further and further. He wished he could look and satisfy himself without staring, without drawing attention to himself, without Susan thinking that he was being obnoxious. Those eyes held mysteries and mischief. Those eyes held pain. Jim wished that he could look into those eyes and wipe away the hurt that he saw there.

Jim caught movement in the corner of his eye. He turned his head and saw a squirrel scampering down a tree. He had to get his mind off Susan. He just couldn't understand how he could be totally captivated by someone he had known less than a day. He didn't know anything about her except that she was a widow and that she was impulsive. Why else would she have shown up on Andrea and George's steps without letting them know ahead of time that she was coming? Still, there was something about her that made him feel that he would like to be able to hold her and soothe the worries, fears and frustrations away.

Jim settled down into his tree stand. It looked as though it would be a perfect morning for enjoying the great outdoors.

Chapter 7

Andrea awoke. She didn't hear anything in the cabin. She looked at her watch; it was a quarter before eight. One of the things she enjoyed about going hunting with George was sleeping in. To get up in the morning without an alarm clock—to lie in bed the extra fifteen to twenty minutes and be lazy—was something she didn't get to do often.

She lay there wondering if George had seen any deer yet, wondering who would be the first to bring in a deer, wondering about Susan. Thinking about Susan made her think of herself and what she wanted to do. She wanted to shoot a deer today. Quickly, she jumped up and made her way to the bathroom. When she had finished with her toiletries, she went to the kitchen and looked to see if there was anything left of the breakfast the men had made earlier.

She heard a door squeak, and when she turned to look she saw Martha coming out of her bedroom. Martha grinned. "Good morning," she said. "I was just waiting until I heard somebody else up before I got up. Well, did the men leave us anything to eat?"

Andrea laughed. "I'm sure we have enough food to not go hungry. It looks like we have some pancake batter left over in the refrigerator and some sausages. I'll put them on."

The women stood in the kitchen while Andrea made the pancakes and put the sausages in the skillet. These mornings were relaxing. Andrea and Martha had fallen into a routine for these mornings over the years, and they both looked forward to them.

"So, what is it with Susan?" Martha asked. "How did she end up coming on the trip?"

Andrea put her fingers to her mouth. "She showed up on our doorstep right before we were supposed to leave," she whispered. "I couldn't leave her there, so we told her to come along."

"You didn't know she was coming?"

"No. She lost her husband two years ago, and it has been a couple of rough years for her. She has struggled emotionally and spiritually, fighting and trying to get a hold of life. She hasn't been able to move on, to live."

Martha's eyes widened. She suddenly understood the kindness that Andrea and George had exhibited in extending their compassion to let Susan be a part of their vacation fun. Martha started to ask more, but just then they heard the bedroom door open. Susan came out.

"Good morning, ladies," she said. "Am I too late?"

"No, you're not too late," said Martha. "Breakfast is ready to be served."

Susan walked over to the stove where Andrea was rolling the sausage links. When Andrea saw her, she gasped. "Susan, who hit you?"

"Huh?" Susan questioned.

"Who hit you?" Andrea asked again.

"Nobody hit me, I guess," Susan said. Suddenly, her visit to the bathroom in the middle of the night came back to her, and she felt the pain on her eyebrows. She put her finger to the one that was all puffy. Oooh, it was sore.

"Yes, somebody hit you," Andrea said. "How else did you get that in the middle of the night?"

"Oh, my," said Martha, "you did get tagged. Who's the guilty culprit? What did you do?"

Susan was flustered. "I . . . I just went to the bathroom," she said. "I went in the dark so that I wouldn't disturb anybody."

"Who . . . what did you hit?" Andrea asked. She walked closer to Susan and gently put her fingers on Susan's eyebrow.

"Ouch," Susan said.

"We need to get some ice on that," Andrea stated matter-of-factly. "Did you hit the door? What did you do?"

Susan looked at Andrea and Martha and hung her head slightly. "I hit Jim," she whispered.

"You did *what*?" Andrea and Martha exclaimed together.

"I hit Jim."

"You hit him? Did he hit you back? What in the world is going on?"

"We collided," Susan explained. "It was dark. We didn't know the other person was there."

"Wait a minute," Andrea said. "Now, tell me again. What in the world happened?"

"I had to go to the bathroom and I didn't want to wake anyone, so I got up quietly and didn't turn on the lights. I thought I would sneak into the bathroom. Anyway, I had to go, and just as I got to the door, I ran into Jim. He was coming out of the bathroom and didn't see me, and I didn't see him."

Andrea looked at Susan's face again. "Well, you're not going to die, are you?"

"Die from being mortified," Susan said. "I feel terrible. I guess he thinks I'm a real klutz."

Andrea laughed, and Martha chuckled. "You two," Andrea said. "You are both so funny. You can't keep your eyes off him . . . you run into him . . . he can't keep his eyes off you . . ."

"He kept me from falling," Susan said. "His arms were so strong. He was so apologetic. I'm afraid I embarrassed him."

Andrea laughed more. The more she thought about and realized what had happened, the harder she laughed. Martha began to laugh harder as well. "Oh, boy," she said, "won't we have stories to tell."

Susan was in a state of panic. "Don't rib him too hard," she pleaded. "I'm so embarrassed. I don't know how to act."

"Don't worry, Susan," said Andrea. "We won't kill him, but we sure won't let him forget it."

The women sat down and began to eat their breakfast. Every time that Andrea glanced at Susan, she cracked up. Susan sat there with a pouty look on her face. She certainly didn't think it was funny. Her eye hurt.

"As I suggested earlier, we need to put some ice on that eye," Andrea said. "But we need to get a picture of it first."

"No! No pictures!" Susan wailed.

"Yes, yes, we need to get a good picture of this so we can blackmail Jim. We can put it up on the church's bulletin board: 'Assistant pastor bashes strange woman.'"

Martha started cackling. Susan put her hand to her mouth, horrified.

"Don't worry," Andrea said. "Jim can take a lot of ribbing. Wait until we get his story. Then we'll really see what happened."

Susan threw her hands in the air in frustration. Had she killed her wonderful week? Had her blunder turned the tide and made the next couple of days too difficult to bear?

Andrea looked over at Martha. "I brought my gun along," she said. Her eyes twinkled with restrained excitement and a touch of mischief.

"You did?" Martha asked. "Are you actually going to put one over on those guys?"

"I'm going to try," Andrea said.

Martha nodded before getting up from the table. "Well, I need to run home and check on a few things, but I'll be back by 11 o'clock to get some lunch ready for the men—I mean, for the hunters—when they come in. I won't be needing your help. We'll eat at noon." With one last knowing glance at Andrea, Martha began clearing the table. The twinkle in Martha's eyes, mixed with her calm manner, only fueled the enthusiasm that was bubbling inside Andrea for her mission.

Susan looked at Andrea. She could sense the stirring of an adventure. Even though she felt rather timid about being out in the woods and surrounded by animals and insects and who knows what else, she knew she didn't want to miss out. She would just have to put on a brave front. So as not to lose her chance or her nerve, and with a look of uncertainty mixed with fear and desperation in her widened eyes, she quickly blurted out, "You want me to go along?"

"Can you sit still?"

Susan was relieved. Andrea hadn't said no. But now she wasn't sure if she had the courage to follow through if Andrea said yes. What had she gotten herself into? She sat up straight, her chin in the air. "Yes, I can sit still," she said. Then, with a little less confidence, she added, "Will I freeze?"

Andrea could see the battle going on in Susan's mind, but she didn't let on to her friend. "Remember," she said, "we brought extra hunting clothes for you. You'll stay plenty warm enough."

Susan thought about it for a while. Her choices seemed rather bleak. If she didn't accompany Andrea, she could either go with Martha, whom she didn't know very well, or stay at the cabin by herself. The first option didn't seem appealing to her, and she also hated the thought of being alone the whole morning. With her thoughts banging between her ears, she decided that the only choice that seemed halfway attractive was to go with Andrea. "If you don't think I'll mess you up, I will go with you," she said.

"Great! Let's get dressed and go." Andrea looked at Susan. Her friend still seemed to be struggling with the idea, so she decided to kick things into high gear. "We can put all of our garb on now and quietly sneak out there. We only have to walk several hundred yards from the cabin, so we shouldn't get hot and sweaty. We'll take some cushions, as we'll be sitting on the ground. The main thing is to be still and quiet. That's better accomplished when you're prepared and comfortable."

Susan still couldn't believe what she was doing. Yesterday morning at this time, when she was driving to George and Andrea's house, she never would have guessed in a million years what she would be doing just twenty-four hours later.

As Andrea and Susan got dressed, they heard Martha leave. They hoped that they would have a story to tell her the next time they saw her. Andrea grabbed her .270 rifle and checked to make sure that she had a knife and shells. She pinned her hunting license on the back of her exterior coat so that she would be in compliance with the Pennsylvania hunting laws. Then she and Susan pulled on their boots. When they were ready, Andrea looked at Susan and said, "Okay, great huntress with the big black eye, let's go hunting!"

Susan looked at her and grinned. Then she wrinkled her nose, put her hand to her eyebrow and quietly said, "Ouch."

"Remember," Andrea said, "sit still and no talking."

The women quietly made their way around and over the small ridge that rose behind the cabin and then started down the other side to where there were a couple of thickets on both sides of the draw. Andrea had sat there during previous trips to get away and enjoy the peace and quiet of the woods by herself. Almost every year, she had seen a buck cross that way. She hoped this morning would be no exception. Oh, how she would sing a song of jubilation and taunt the men if she were able to hang a deer on that meat pole before anyone else.

The women eased into a soft, concave spot in the ground in front of a couple of rocks. The year before, Andrea had worked hard to put some thick brush and other rocks in front of this spot to help hide it. She had been planning for several years to pull off this coup. She looked at Susan, grinned, and mouthed the words, "This will be fun."

Susan looked at her and wondered exactly what was going to be fun. She had never spent time in the woods. It was a whole new concept for her. And what about Andrea carrying a gun? Would she actually shoot something? Susan couldn't believe what she was witnessing, but she was up for it.

Andrea rested the gun over the brush in front of her so that it would steady the rifle if she had the chance to shoot a deer. Satisfied that everything was in place, Andrea leaned back against the rock and breathed a sigh of contentment. Susan looked at her and, following suit, also sighed and sat back against the rock.

"Now what?" Susan whispered.

"Shh," Andrea said. "Now we stay quiet. We wait. We sit still. We listen."

They sat for five minutes. Susan just couldn't comprehend the art of hunting. She slowly turned her head toward Andrea and, with a crooked grin on her face, asked, "Are we having fun?" She could see the twinkle in Andrea's eyes. Her friend quietly formed the word "yes" on her lips.

They sat and waited. A squirrel played in front of them, and then another squirrel joined in. The woods became noisy as the squirrels chased each other up the tree and down the tree. Susan closed her eyes, wondering how long this would take, wondering what she was doing here. Her hand went to her eyebrow. Andrea quietly reached over, touched her on the arm and said, "Shh. No movement. We need to be still."

Susan looked at Andrea. "I am," she said.

"No, you're not," Andrea said. "We need to sit *still*."

Susan sat back and closed her eyes. If this was fun, she would hate to see what they called boredom.

Unexpectedly, Susan heard Andrea hiss, "Shh! Be still!" Susan's eyes popped wide open. She couldn't believe it! Forty yards in front of them she caught movement on the edge of the thicket, and then out stepped a deer. Slowly, Andrea brought the gun into position. Susan was horrified. Time seemed to stand still, and she wondered what would happen next. The doe stepped forward, and another younger deer stepped out behind it. They walked down the trail, crisscrossing the small ravine before going up the other side. It took the deer four to five minutes to go the fifty yards. Susan sat still, petrified, not knowing what to expect.

Finally, the deer were out of sight. Susan couldn't contain herself. "Why didn't you shoot?" she said.

"Shh!" Andrea said. "They were does, and I only have a buck tag. There have to be at least three points on one side. Shh, Susan. A lot of times a buck will follow a doe."

Susan was keyed up. She hadn't seen a deer that close before. She thought of Bambi. He was so cute, so lovable, with his eyes so big and so brown. How could anyone kill a deer? She thought about what Andrea had said. *I'm glad you weren't bucks,* she thought. *That way, you're able to live.*

Just then, they heard some shots in the distance. Andrea looked at Susan. "That sounded like Jim shooting," she said.

"How do you know?" Susan asked.

"Because of the ridge from which the shot came. We need to hurry up, get my buck and bring it back to the cabin before he brings his in."

"You're talking, Andrea. Why are you talking when you told me to be quiet?"

Andrea showed Susan a lopsided grin. "You're right. Shh. Let's be quiet."

Susan sat back, but she didn't close her eyes. It was pure elation for her to see deer, and she wondered what would happen if a buck did walk out. Suddenly, she caught motion again off in the distance. Out of the corner of her eye, she saw Andrea tense, lean forward and position the gun. Susan watched as the deer stepped out of the thicket and into the open woods. This deer had antlers on its head. Andrea, very attentively, watched the deer through the scope of her rifle.

Susan glanced at Andrea. Why wasn't she shooting? Half of her was rooting for the deer to hurry up and run across to the thicket on the other side, while the other half of her wanted to see Andrea pull off her stunt and beat the men.

The deer had almost made it across the small draw and was getting ready to enter the woods on the other side. Andrea still hadn't taken a shot. Susan's nerves were on edge with the anticipation of the moment. Just as the deer was getting ready to step into the thicket, Susan again caught motion and looked back down the trail. A much bigger buck was stepping out of the thicket onto the trail. It stood three-fourths of the way out, with its head held high, looking directly at Susan and at Andrea. Susan froze and held her breath. She couldn't believe such a gorgeous animal was so close, boring its eyes into her, as if it could read her very thoughts.

At the crack of the rifle, Susan jumped, ducked, covered her ears and let out a squeal. The big buck had spun around and run back into the brush. Susan had never heard anything so loud. Realizing what she had done, she quickly clasped her hands to her mouth. After her heart had stopped pounding in her chest and the commotion of startled birds and running deer had subsided, she whipped her head around to look at Andrea. "Why didn't you tell me you were going to shoot?" she hissed, not sure if her frantic tone of voice was a product of fright, frustration or excitement.

"I didn't have time," Andrea breathed, not noticing Susan's tone. Apart from a pair of scampering squirrels, the woods were again completely quiet, though the shot still rang in her ears. There was no reason to talk quietly now, but somehow the moment seemed sacred. "It spied us, and I either had to shoot right then or not get the shot off at all." Andrea barely spoke above a whisper, but as she continued to peer through the woods, she couldn't conceal the thrill of victory in her voice.

Susan's question reminded Andrea of the task at hand, and she slowly drew her gaze away from the woods in the direction the buck had run. She turned and smiled at Susan. "Come on. Let's gather our things."

"Did you get it?" Susan asked. "It ran off." She couldn't understand the gleam in Andrea's eyes. After all, the deer was nowhere to be seen. How could Andrea seem so excited when, as far as she could tell, if Andrea did indeed hit the deer, it would be next to impossible to find?

Andrea looked at her and grinned. Then she jumped to her feet and in a belated emotional outburst exclaimed, "Oh, I think I got my deer!"

"It ran off," Susan said again, still feeling perplexed.

"It won't run far," Andrea assured her. "I had those crosshairs right on his front shoulder, and at forty yards, with my steady aim, I know I didn't miss."

"So what do we do now?" Susan asked. She still couldn't believe that Andrea had shot a deer.

Andrea carefully loaded another shell into the rifle. "Let's sit for a couple of minutes so that we can calm down and give the deer time to expire. We'll go to where it was on the trail and see if we can find blood."

"Oh," Susan groaned, "you shot Bambi."

Andrea looked at her and laughed. "Yes, and it will make good eating, too. There are much bigger deer in the woods, but this is a nice one."

Andrea picked up the rifle and carefully got up. With Susan in tow behind her, she quietly snuck down to the trail where they had last seen the deer at the edge of the thicket. When they got to the deer trail, Andrea looked around. At first, she didn't see anything, so she carefully took several steps forward, scanning with her eyes and peering at the ground.

"Blood," Andrea whispered. "Good, Susan, I hit him. I knew I got him. Let's just carefully follow this blood trail out. Stay behind me, Susan, in case the animal is still alive."

Andrea followed the trail carefully. At first the blood appeared in small blotches, and then, as the deer bled profusely, in larger pools. They traveled about thirty yards and topped a small rise. Abruptly, Andrea stopped and brought the rifle to her shoulder. She peered through the scope at the deer that lay in front of her. It was very dead.

Andrea turned and looked at Susan with a big grin on her face. "We did it, Susan!" she all but squealed. "Now the fun begins! Come and look! Come help me!"

Susan cautiously came up behind Andrea and peered around her to catch a glimpse of the deer. "Oh, my!" she said, feeling rather timid. All at once, she was consciously aware of how out of place she felt. "It's Bambi!"

"No, not Bambi," Andrea said. "This is a mature buck. He could be bigger, but he will do. The men will have a fit!"

Andrea cautiously moved forward and lightly touched the animal's eye with the barrel of her .270 rifle. "Yippee!" she squealed, jumping up and down. She took the shell out of her gun, propped the rifle up against a tree, and turned back to her deer.

Susan, half mortified, stared down at the animal. "Why? Why did you do it, Andrea?" she asked, feeling awkwardly emotional about Andrea shooting such a beautiful animal.

"Oh, there are numerous reasons," Andrea said cheerfully. Seeing the concern on her friend's face, she decided to try to boost Susan's spirits and give her a balanced perspective. "One reason is for food. Most likely, this is a two-and-a-half-year-old buck. Let's count the points. One, two, three, four on this side and, yes, four on the other side. A beautiful, symmetrical, fifteen-inch-wide, eight-point buck. The guys will be envious of me. This is not an old deer. The meat will be great for eating, nice and tender."

"Oh, my," Susan said. "What a beautiful deer."

"You're quite right, Susan," Andrea replied. "It is a beautiful deer. A wonderful creature that God created for us to enjoy and to provide us with a source of food. It helps complete the cycle of life. The deer eats leaves, we eat the deer, and, when we pass on, we'll help nourish the leaves."

Susan shuddered. She carefully went up and touched the deer on the forehead. "It is kind of cute," she said quietly.

"Not cute. Just plain beautiful," Andrea remarked. "What a wonderful deer. Now for the real fun!"

"What do you mean?" Susan asked. She was not sure she wanted to hear the answer.

Andrea grinned. "Well, we need to pull it out of this thicket so we can get around it, and then we need to field dress it, and then we need to get it back to the camp and on that meat pole before the men get there."

Susan looked at Andrea, and then back at the deer. "That's a lot of work," she said, wrinkling up her nose. "What are you going to do?"

Andrea grinned. "Here. I'll show you. Help me." She grabbed hold of one of the antlers and started to pull and twist the deer around. "Help me, Susan."

"Help you?" Susan asked, glancing down at her gloved hands that were awkwardly, yet comfortably, snuggled into her much-too-large wool mittens.

"Grab hold of the other antler," Andrea said. "The two of us should be able to pull it out of the thicket." Susan carefully took hold of the antler with one gloved hand and started to tug at it. "Don't pull gently, Susan. We have to work together. Use both hands and pull hard."

Together, they tugged and pulled the deer out of the thicket, into the open woods, and back on to the trail that had led the deer to his demise. "Let's point his head up the hill," instructed Andrea. They swung the deer around and pulled it forward so that its hind legs were pointing down the draw.

"Now what?" Susan asked, panting. "That's hard work!"

"Well, we can lighten it by about ten pounds."

"Lighten it? What do you mean?"

"It's time to field dress it."

"Field dress it?" Susan shuddered. She didn't know what that meant, but she didn't think she was going to like it. She was already in way over her head, and she had endured about all the excitement a city girl could handle in the woods for one day. She just wanted to get back to the cabin, fill her growling stomach with whatever Martha had prepared for lunch, and curl up with a book in a chair next to the warm stove.

"Yes," Andrea remarked as she pulled out her hunting knife and went to the tail end of the deer. "Here. Hold these legs apart."

Susan looked on in shock as Andrea began to cut open the deer. "Come on, Susan," she said. "You're a nurse. You've certainly seen this kind of thing before."

Andrea slit the deer's belly and, rolling up her sleeves, worked at removing all of the insides so the meat wouldn't spoil before they were able to get it to the butcher's. Susan stood and just blinked, a grimace growing on her face. "I can't believe you're doing this," she said.

"All in a day's work," Andrea said with a grin.

Ten minutes later, Andrea wiped the knife off on the leaves and looked up at Susan. "Now, to the creek so we can wash our hands and clean the knife."

"This is horrible!" Susan exclaimed.

Andrea laughed, her eyes still twinkling. "It may look horrible, but it's going to melt in your mouth! Just you wait and see."

Andrea went down to the small stream of water and washed off her knife, and then washed off her hands and arms. The water was cold, but it made her feel good. She had accomplished something that she had been dreaming of doing for several years. The elation of showing the men the deer she had shot was beginning to build within her. She felt she could almost burst with the anticipation.

Andrea walked back up to the deer. "Now what?" Susan asked.

"Now we pull," Andrea said. "Pull it the same way we did to get it out of the thicket."

The two women pulled the deer all of twenty-five feet and then stopped. Susan looked at Andrea. "Okay, now what?" she asked.

"Plan B," Andrea came back. "Let's take the gun and all of our supplies back down to the cabin. That will relieve us of a bunch of weight. Then we can come back and get the deer."

The women went the several hundred yards up over the ridge and down to the cabin, where they deposited their things. Andrea hoped that Martha would be back so that the three of them, together, would be able to drag the deer. After all, many hands make light work, and six hands could more easily get that deer up and down the small ridge than four. But when they arrived at the cabin, they quickly discovered that Martha had not yet come back to start dinner.

"We can do this," Andrea said.

They went back over the ridge and down to the deer. Andrea and Susan each grabbed hold of one antler and started pulling again, stopping every forty or fifty feet to rest. Forty-five minutes later, they had the deer lying on the ground underneath the meat pole.

Susan flopped down on the ground. "I'm exhausted! That is hard work!"

Andrea could hardly keep from giggling. "You bet it's hard work, but just think of the fun we're going to have with this!" She went around to the edge of the cabin where the water hose was hooked up to the faucet. Uncoiling the hose, she brought it back to the deer and, after turning the water on, opened the legs of the deer so that she could spray water into the deer cavity.

"Watch that water spray, Susan, I don't want you to get wet," Andrea said. "Now hold the buck up by the antlers so the water will run out." Susan did as she was told, and Andrea washed out the deer.

When she was finished, Andrea said, "Now we need to get it strung up on the meat pole."

"How are we going to do that?" Susan asked.

Andrea went into the cabin and got a ratchet rope, and then went down to the basement to get a high stepladder. She brought it back out and leaned it up against the edge of the meat pole so that she could reach the top. She took the small rope, tied it loosely around the pole, and then put the metal hook of the ratchet rope in the loop. Finally, she took a small stick and pushed the loop of rope further away, toward the middle of the meat pole.

"Okay, now we're ready," she said as she climbed back down the ladder.

The two women pulled the deer close, just below where the rope was. Susan looked up. "How are we going to do this?" she asked.

"Simple." Andrea said. "Here, you hold the head up and I will circle the neck with the rope and attach it to itself. Then all we have to do is get on the other end of the rope and pull. It will be easy."

Susan reluctantly took hold of the deer. Never in one day had she had to overcome so many mental obstacles accompanied by mental anguish and stomach-turning disgust. This was all so new to her, so, so . . . out of her comfort zone. "Oh! I'm getting all wet! Oooooh, this is terrible! How can you kill such an animal and then make me hold it?"

Andrea looked at her and smiled. "Just keep holding it like that." She went around the deer, jumped up and reached the top end of the rope. When she pulled, Susan felt the weight of the deer ease out of her hands.

"Okay, Susan," Andrea said. "Grab a bit lower down and pull up on the deer again, and I'll pull on the rope."

Susan squirmed. She had had no idea what she was getting into when she agreed to go on this hunt. She could not imagine seeing herself doing what she was doing.

Again Andrea pulled on the rope, and gradually hoisted the deer up about four feet off the ground.

"Whew, I'm tired," Susan said. "Are we done?"

"Not quite," Andrea replied. "I need to find a twenty-inch stick."

"A twenty-inch stick? Where are we going to find that?"

"Somewhere thereabouts," Andrea said, pointing off toward the woods. "We need to put the stick between its hind legs to hold them apart. That will help to cool the meat off so that it won't spoil."

Susan shook her head. "You find the stick. I'll take the stepladder back to the basement."

"Agreed," Andrea answered.

Andrea soon found a stick in the trees and broke it so it was the right length. She put it between the legs of the deer, stood back and smiled. They would take pictures later when the men came back to camp, but first she wanted to get that deer hanging from the meat pole and remove all of the evidence. She took the water hose, rolled it back up and laid it against the cabin. Susan came back from putting the stepladder away.

"Let's go into the cabin," Andrea said. "I'm ready for a snack."

"I'm ready to get cleaned up!" Susan said with a grimace. "I've never looked or smelled like this since forever."

Andrea just smiled and walked into the cabin. They took off their outer layers and washed up. "Now, for a cup of coffee and a little snack," Andrea said. She looked over at Susan and their eyes met. The thrill of victory and the satisfaction of a challenge—of a dream fulfilled—hung in the air between them.

"Oh, give me a hug, Susan!" Andrea exclaimed. She grabbed Susan, and they twirled around laughing. "I am so excited!"

Although Susan still felt bewildered, a strange feeling of pride, mixed with self-confidence, began to grow inside of her. She put her hand on her head. She couldn't believe what she had experienced and what she had accomplished in the last day and a half.

The women each got a cup of coffee and some vanilla wafers and then sat down at the table to await the men's arrival. Susan was silent, but Andrea couldn't sit still. She kept getting up and going over to look out the window at the deer hanging on the meat pole. Her first deer, and they had pulled it off without the men even knowing they were going to be out hunting. She felt triumphant in her scheming and planning.

They were sitting and sipping their coffee when they heard a vehicle drive up. The girls hurried to the window and looked out to see who it was. It was Martha, coming back from her home. She stopped and looked at the deer, walked over to it, and then came into the cabin. "Which one of the men is bragging now?" she asked.

"It isn't a man bragging," Susan said, feeling smug and playful. "We're the ones who are bragging!"

"You? What? What do you mean?" Martha asked.

Throughout the day Susan had been uncomfortable, but she suddenly felt victorious and boastful as she began to glimpse the coup that Andrea was pulling off. "No man killed that buck," she said.

"What do you mean?" Martha asked again. She looked from Susan to Andrea. The telltale signs on Andrea's face, grin and all, made her stop. "Don't tell me you did it!" she exclaimed, unloading the bags in her arms and showing more emotion than normal.

"I sure did," Andrea responded.

"Where, how, when . . . oh, mercy! Now, you've done it!" Martha could hardly contain herself. With one hand she covered her gaping mouth, as if to hide her excitement should the men show up at that very moment and feel offended at her pleasure in the ladies one-upping them, and with the other she reached for the counter as if to steady herself from the shocking news.

Andrea laughed. "I hope I've done it. We've pulled a good one on those men. They won't believe this."

Martha was determined not to start lunch until she had gotten a good look at the soon-to-be-famous deer. She walked out of the cabin with Andrea and Susan to look at the prize. The sun was beginning to feel warm overhead, and they savored the moment as they stood in front of the deer, enjoying the jubilation and the fun that they would have when the men came in from their morning hunt.

"They normally come in around noon to eat lunch," Andrea said. "What time is it now, anyway?"

"Eleven-thirty," Martha said, looking at her watch. "Let's go in and get some sandwiches for those men. This is going to be a riot!"

Andrea hugged herself with delight. She just could hardly wait for the men to come back.

"I wonder if they got anything," Martha said.

"We heard some shots at different places this morning," Andrea remarked. "We couldn't tell for sure, though, if any of them came from our men."

"I hope they didn't," Susan responded. "That would just be too good. Here we are, the great huntresses, and our poor men can't even do anything."

Andrea looked at Martha. Somehow, Susan was starting to come out of her defensive posturing and was beginning to feel the current of electricity in the atmosphere.

The women went back into the kitchen and got out the cold cuts to prepare lunch. Twenty minutes later, the women heard a vehicle drive up. They rushed to the window and peeked out. The men rolled out of the Jeep Cherokee and walked over to the deer, looking at it and pointing.

Jim turned to George. "Okay, wise guys, which one of you all pulled a fast one this morning?"

"That's what I'd like to know," George returned. He looked at Sam.

"Don't look at me!" Sam said indignantly.

Jim looked toward the cabin and saw the women's faces disappear from behind the curtain. Instantly, he had a funny feeling. He glanced over at George again. "Are you telling me that's not your deer?" he asked.

"Not my deer," George quipped.

Jim looked at Sam.

"Don't look at me," Sam repeated. "I saw some does and a couple of spikes, but nothing legal to shoot."

"Well gentlemen, it certainly is not my deer," Jim replied. "Somehow, we have a deer on the meat pole, and those gals know something about it. I just saw them duck behind the curtain in the cabin."

"Oh, mercy," George said. "I don't like the picture of what I'm beginning to see here. If this is what I think it is, we'll never live this one down!"

Jim grinned. "But who? Which one?"

"Which one would?" asked George.

"Well, certainly not Susan," Jim responded.

"Now, how do you know so much about Susan all of a sudden?"

"Well, it can't be her, not the way that she . . ."

"Okay, okay, we know," said George.

"It couldn't have been Martha," Sam said. "She lamented last week about not buying a hunting license this year, and I don't believe she bought a license this past week, so I'm sure it's not her."

They both looked at George.

"Well, if it was Andrea, I certainly don't know anything about it," he said. "I didn't know that she had bought a license. But, well, I don't know." George shook his head. "How could she . . . well, what gun would she have used? She, she couldn't have . . ."

The men looked at each other and then looked at the door of the cabin. The women, in their eagerness, were not able to wait any longer. The door opened, and the three of them stood in the doorway.

"Okay, mighty hunters, where are your deer?"

George looked at the ladies and then at Jim and Sam.

"Yes, where are the great hunters and all of your conquests? What do you have to show for yourselves?" Susan was enjoying watching the plot thicken as the men stared at them. She was the outsider, but somehow that made her feel as though she was in the driver's seat. She was on the outside looking in at the story that was being played out in front of her eyes.

"How did that deer get there?" Jim asked.

"It just came bounding out of the woods and took a big leap and hung itself," Martha said.

The men again looked at the deer. It was an eight-pointer with a fifteen-inch spread. "Somebody got a nice deer," Jim said.

The women came out of the cabin and walked over toward them.

"Yep," Andrea said, "somebody sure did get a nice deer. I just wonder who in the world . . . which one of you men snuck out of the woods this morning and brought that deer in here?"

"Okay, wise guy—er, wise lady," George responded. "What gives? What's going on? Where did that deer come from?"

"I had chores to do this morning," Martha said. "I haven't been hunting."

"I just showed up," Susan remarked. "Remember? Yesterday at dinnertime. I didn't even know I was going to be here. That clears me."

The men all stared at Andrea. She couldn't keep the grin off her face. "Yeah, well, like I said, somebody has to supply some meat around here."

"What did you do?" George asked. "How did you do this? Do you have a license?"

"Do I have a license?" Andrea asked, feigning shock at the question. "George, shame on you. You know I wouldn't shoot a deer illegally."

"You did shoot it, then?" George asked.

"Sure, she shot it," Susan chirped in. "And I sat there and watched her!"

"You did *what*?" Jim asked.

"Yep, I sat right there and watched her," Susan said again.

"Well, where was the deer?" Jim asked.

"Shh!" Andrea said. "Susan, don't tell them where I got it!"

"I can tell you that it wasn't a long walk," Susan said. Andrea glared at her with a look of exasperation on her face. She didn't want her hidden spot to be revealed.

Jim watched Andrea, and then Susan. "I'm hungry," he said, "but okay, wise young lady. You follow me." He took a walk around the edge of the small lawn where the cabin sat. He immediately looked up to the ridge behind the cabin in the small hollow leading up to the top of the ridge several hundred yards away.

"What are you doing, Jim?" Susan asked.

Jim raised an eyebrow. "That's okay. You already told me you walked. We'll find out where you got that deer." He walked to the bottom of the small draw that led up to the saddle in the ridge. It didn't take him long to find where the deer had been dragged out of the woods.

"Why are you going this way?" Susan asked.

Jim looked at her. "I'm not 'the great tracker' for nothing," he said. "Follow me."

Andrea looked appalled as Jim started up the draw, with Susan walking behind him. Jim followed the trail and the drops of blood. When he got to the top, he looked down and could immediately see where the deer had been dragged up the ridge.

"You gals had a workout this morning, didn't you?" he said, turning to look at Susan. Susan glanced at him and looked around. Suddenly, she realized that the two of them were alone together. Her cockiness, just as quickly as it had come, started to melt away.

"A lot of hard work," she said quietly.

Jim continued down the other side and soon reached the trail that crisscrossed in the small hollow. "Here," he said. "Here's where you field dressed it." He looked and saw the trails. Walking over to the edge of the thicket, he took a few steps in and saw the blood on the trail. He looked back up to the top of the mountain and then started off at a strong gait, eyes searching and looking—looking and searching. About forty yards up, he stopped.

"Ah, ha!" he exclaimed. "So here's where you were sitting!"

"How did you do that?" Susan asked.

"Do what?"

"Find Andrea's secret deer stand."

Jim laughed. "So this is where she got it. When you leave a trail that wide open, anyone can follow it."

Susan felt frustrated and let down. Now that they knew where Andrea had killed her deer, would they try to take it from her? She looked at Jim. "You're too much! This is Andrea's spot!"

"It's a good one," Jim said. "She's a wise lady to figure out where to sit, and she certainly didn't have far to go from the cabin. Here we men go out in the big woods trying to kill our deer, and she sneaks out behind the cabin and kills a nice buck. Give credit where credit is due. She certainly has pulled a fast one on us."

Susan glanced at Jim and again to where she and Andrea had sat that morning. She pictured herself and Jim sitting there with their shoulders rubbing.

"What are you smiling at?" Jim asked.

Susan blinked and gave a slight shake of her head. She had to get a grip on herself. She had to keep Jim at a distance. Somehow, the emotions that were creeping into her inner being didn't feel right. They didn't feel right to someone who had lost her husband and who had mourned continuously for the past two years. They didn't feel right to someone who had spent the last two years in a state of sorrow, denial, anger and frustration, just trying to cope.

"Let's get back to the cabin," Jim said. "I'm hungry, and I don't want those other guys to eat all of our food." He turned and started to take long steps, up the draw, to the top of the mountain. Susan started to follow after him but was soon fifteen to twenty feet behind him. Jim, realizing that she wasn't keeping up, slowed down.

"Are you tired, Susan?" he asked.

"Yes, I'm very tired," Susan said. "It was a lot of hard work for us to pull that deer up out of here."

Jim softened. "Yes, I'm sure it was. That was a lot of work. You two should have waited for us men to help you."

Susan grinned. "That was part of the fun! Getting that deer on the meat pole for you all to see when you came back to the cabin." She stopped. She took deep breaths, trying to get enough oxygen into her lungs so she could continue up the ridge.

"Here, let me help you," Jim said, noticing her discomfort. He reached out his hand, grabbed hold of Susan's and started helping her up the ridge. When he took her hand, a shock went through him.

Susan looked down at her hand in Jim's, and in her innermost being she sighed. Somehow, it didn't feel wrong to feel Jim's hand in hers. It was a feeling she needed, a feeling she had lacked the past couple of years, a feeling that helped her feel more whole. With renewed energy, she continued walking until they reached the top of the ridge. Once they were there, Jim lessened his grip and started to let go of Susan's hand, but Susan wasn't ready, yet, to lose the connection. She wanted to keep that sense of satisfaction and spark of hope that stirred inside her for as long as possible. Jim looked into her eyes.

"I guess I can hold your hand going down, too, so you won't run ahead and leave me behind," he said with a smile.

"I'm so tired that I might stumble if you don't hold my hand, Jim," Susan quipped back.

They again stared at each other, and Jim looked deep into Susan's multi-colored brown eyes. "Your eyes," Jim said. "Will you give me permission just to stare into them?"

Susan stopped and smiled. "They're only eyes."

"Eyes like I've never seen before," Jim murmured. He continued to stare and to search and to look into Susan's eyes, eyes that had so much depth, but still couldn't conceal her sorrow and sadness. Finally, he stood back and smiled. "I could get used to looking into those eyes, Susan."

Susan punched her elbow into Jim's side. "Now you're picking on me!"

"Is there anything any better to do?" Jim laughed.

Together, they walked back down the hollow. As they neared the cabin, Susan pulled her hand away from Jim. Jim looked at her, then at the cabin, and quickly realized that Susan didn't want to be seen holding his hand. *That's okay,* he thought to himself. *I don't know what this situation may lead to, but it surely is different.*

In all of Jim's high school and college days he had been shy about dating, and when he had dated, there had never been a girl who had captivated his feelings or his emotions. He was always ill at ease and was never relaxed. Somehow, Susan was different. With the problems she'd had, he wondered why she had come with them on an impulse. Jim had a lot of questions to ask himself, and he looked forward to going back to his tree stand for the evening hunt so he could have some time to think. He needed to work through whether things could be different in a relationship with someone like Susan.

By the time Jim and Susan entered the cabin, everyone had eaten their sandwiches. George lay on the couch, and Sam sat in a recliner. They had a hunting video on, but both men had their eyes closed.

"We made you some sandwiches," Andrea said to Jim and Susan. "I hope you like what we made. I hope you didn't find anything on the ridge."

Jim looked at Andrea and grinned. "I found a couple of things on that ridge, and one is where you shot that deer."

Andrea stuck out her lower lip and pouted. "That was my secret."

"It was a good secret, cousin. You certainly did pull a fast one on us today. How did you get your rifle up here without us knowing it?"

Andrea laughed. "Susan gave me the answer to that one. When we needed to get an extra sleeping bag for her, we just hid the rifle inside."

"Well, you definitely did yourself proud," Jim responded. "Do you have a doe tag?"

"No. I applied, but I was too late and they turned me down. But I'm content—I did what I wanted to do."

"I would say you did indeed."

George opened one eye. He was listening, even though they thought he was asleep. He was thankful that Andrea, his wife, and Jim, her first cousin, were as close as they were. It was good to be married to a wonderful friend, for Jim to be his friend as well, and for the cousins to enjoy and appreciate being with each other. George closed his eyes and continued to rest. He had visions of the evening hunt. With his eyes closed, he said matter-of-factly, "Well, Jim, you're not going to let a cousin beat you, are you?"

Jim waited until his mouth was empty from chewing on his sandwich. "Nope! I've got mine hog-tied up. I'll be getting it this afternoon."

Susan looked at Jim. Secretly, she hoped that he would get his deer. She had mixed emotions about it: she wanted Jim to get one bigger than Andrea, but she also wanted Andrea to have the biggest. As she ate her sandwich and chips and drank her soda, her mind was working in overdrive. She hadn't had this much fun in years.

At 2:30, the men stirred and, again, started their usual banter.

"It's time to go get a big one, boys," said Sam.

"Yep, it's time to go," said George.

"Time to stay in the cabin and rest," Andrea quipped.

"That's right," Susan added. "We worked hard this morning."

The men rolled their eyes, looked at Andrea and Susan, shrugged and put on their wraps.

"I think I'll go right back to where I was this morning," Jim said, talking to no one in particular. "I know that deer travel through there. I'll get mine this evening."

"I think I'll have a good chance," George said. "I saw a four-pointer this morning, along with a couple of spikes and does. Did you say you saw deer this morning, Sam?"

"I saw a couple of does and a young buck."

"Well, sounds like we all saw deer. It's just that not all of us were able to have them fall over our gun barrel and die of a broken heart."

Andrea stuck her tongue out and made a face at George. "Mock me all you like. You see who has what hanging on the meat pole." She laughed.

Susan walked over to the couch, sat down and began to watch the deer video. Twenty-four hours earlier, it would have been of no interest to her at all. In fact, she would have thought it was horrible. Now, she looked at it with a certain sense of curiosity. As she watched a nice buck on the screen, out of the blue, across the audio came the small crack of a rifle. She saw the deer jump and run.

"Oh, no!" she exclaimed. "They shot it."

"That's what you're supposed to do," Jim said. He went out the door.

For the men, the afternoon was more eventful. Jim was in his tree by three o'clock, and he settled down to watch and listen. His mind went back to the hunt in the morning and to the disappointment of not seeing a legal deer. He knew that this evening he had just as good a chance to get a deer as he'd had in the morning. He thought of Andrea harvesting a nice buck. He grinned as he recalled how he had found the place where she had shot the buck.

He thought about Susan's small hand in his as he helped pull her back up the mountain, and then her wanting to continue holding his hand as they came down the other side toward the cabin. Looking up to the heavens, he whispered in an audible voice, "God, what is going on?" He began to again picture Susan's brown eyes—eyes that had so many different colors and into which you could look so deeply. How did this young lady enter his life? What was it about her that drew him? Did he want to be drawn to her? Should he fight it? He tried not to think about her, but, as the afternoon wore on, his thoughts kept going back to how he held her hand and looked into her eyes on the return trip from Andrea's stand.

Jim was sitting there daydreaming, thinking about how he would like to hold Susan's hand again, when suddenly he caught movement and snapped back to reality. He was supposed to be deer hunting. There, in front of him, were a couple of does prancing across the forest floor, getting ready to come out into the alfalfa field to eat. Jim's mind turned back to hunting as he slowly got his rifle into a position where he could shoot if a buck were to follow.

The does broke out of the edge of the woods and started feeding in the alfalfa. It looked to Jim as if there were five deer: two does and that year's offspring. He carefully raised his rifle and looked at the deer through his scope. When he saw the knobs on two of the three young deer, he smiled. They were button bucks, and they would help to secure hunting a couple of years down the road. He lowered his rifle.

He continued to sit there and watch the deer, listening and scanning the woods with his eyes. Unexpectedly, he again caught motion. A couple more deer were filtering out of the thicket into the open woods and heading toward the alfalfa field. The first he saw was another doe, but the second one behind the doe caused him to stop and look. Even without the help of binoculars or the rifle scope, he could see that it was a nice-racked buck. "There have to be three points on one side," he reminded himself.

He carefully raised his rifle and scoped the buck. He counted five points on one side, and after that he didn't worry about the horns or the rack. Instead, he raised his head just enough to watch the deer above his scope. It slowly made its way closer to the alfalfa field and then stopped. Jim's pulse began to race as he realized that he was looking at a nice deer. As many deer as he had shot, the passion for and thrill of the hunt never dimmed, nor did the realization of being able to harvest such a beautiful animal.

The deer began to move slowly and, when the buck again stopped, Jim had a clear view of it. He carefully planted the cross hairs on the scope tight up against the front shoulder of the deer, and then he continued to move midway up its body. The deer took another step forward. Its side was now toward Jim and its front leg was forward. Jim smiled and moved the cross hairs two inches toward the front of the deer. It was a perfect shot placement. He steadied the gun on the rest in front of him, took a breath, quietly exhaled and started applying pressure on the trigger. The "sight" picture continued to look good. Jim tried not to bat his eyes and continued to squeeze the gun trigger. Suddenly, the recoil of the gun responded.

Jim saw the buck wheel and run, its tail tucked tight between its legs. He racked another shell into the gun and watched as the deer disappeared back into the mountain laurel thicket. The deer in the alfalfa field that had been in front and in back of the buck turned and ran, their white tails waving as they bounded and crisscrossed each other back into the woods.

Jim sat there in stunned silence. He had just killed one of the nicest deer of his life. Peace and quiet were again surrounding him. He knew that the mood swings of the forest were peace and quiet, with deer feeding, and then, suddenly, a second of disturbance, and then peace and quiet again.

As Jim sat there, he realized that he had accomplished what he had set out to do in Pennsylvania. He laughed a little to himself. Maybe he didn't get the first deer, and the men might have been snookered on the morning hunt, but he certainly believed that he had just gotten a bigger deer than the one that was hanging on the meat pole. He grinned. Now they would be bragging for him. Susan would compliment him for killing a nice deer the way she had been so proud of Andrea.

But what did Susan have to do with it? Jim was happy that he had shot the deer. Yet Susan's face came back to him, and for some reason he wanted very much to have her praise him for what he had done.

Jim waited another ten minutes and then carefully climbed down out of his tree stand. He had made a mental picture as to where the buck had been standing, and he walked up to that spot. He searched a little and found the kicked-up leaves and the deer's sharp footprints in the soft earth. With the shock of the bullet, the deer had automatically recoiled and dug his feet into the ground with the impulse to leap backward and to get out of the way.

Jim looked in the direction in which the deer had run. He could see the leaves scuffed up, revealing the trail where the deer had gone. He could also see red splotches of blood in front of him. He smiled and carefully started walking the trail of his deer.

He found the deer seventy-five yards further up the trail. When Jim saw it, he let out a low whistle. Of all the deer that he had killed, this was unquestionably one of the best. He touched the rifle barrel up against the eyeball of the deer and got no response. Propping his rifle up against a tree, he picked up the deer's head, looked at its antlers and counted the points. It was a perfect ten, with a nineteen-inch inside spread. Jim was elated. Men had hunted a lifetime and never found a deer as mature and nice as this one. As he sat there, the glowing excitement built up within him. This is one deer that would cost him some money; it would have to go on the wall. He had one other deer on the wall, one he had killed four years earlier, but this was another one that would definitely grace his home.

Jim continued to look at the deer, feeling the mass of the antlers. He went to his knapsack and pulled out a camera. He wanted to take some pictures to put in a scrapbook. He wanted to remember this moment for the rest of his life.

As Jim snapped a few pictures, he slowly breathed a prayer of thanks. He thanked God for the privilege of being able to hunt, for the privilege of being able to harvest such a beautiful animal, and for the privilege of having meat to eat. He grinned to himself. He might have to make deer jerky and bologna out of this one—it was old enough that it would be more inclined to have some wild flavor to it. He could figure that out later; right now he just wanted to enjoy the beauty of the buck. He again felt a sense of accomplishment at being able to take down such a beautiful animal.

Jim quickly field dressed the animal and got on his walkie-talkie. "Anybody out there?" he asked. There was no response. He looked at his watch—ten minutes before four. He knew that in ten minutes somebody would be on the walkie-talkie because each hour, on the hour, the hunters made contact if anything important was going on. They used earphones and talked quietly to keep the noise level as low as possible. Jim knew the other guys had heard his shot and would be curious about what had happened.

The stand where Sam had let Jim off was only a half-mile from the cabin. Jim knew he couldn't sit still and wait an hour and a half for darkness to overtake the evening and his deer to be picked up. His excitement had to have movement. He decided to walk to the cabin, get his Cherokee, and retrieve the deer himself.

Jim picked up his backpack and his rifle and started back to the cabin. At four o'clock, he turned on his walkie-talkie.

"Hey, Jim, is that you?" George asked.

"Yeah, it's me," Jim said.

"Do any good?"

"Yeah, did a little good."

"How big?"

"Big enough."

"How big?"

"Big enough to straighten out Andrea."

"Oh, yeah?"

"Must have been a good one," Sam cut in.

"Yeah, good enough," Jim answered.

"I'm going to stay here and hunt until evening," George said.

"I'm just getting back to the cabin," Jim returned. "I thought I'd go ahead and get my Cherokee so I can retrieve the deer and hang it on the meat pole. You guys just remember one thing: when you drive in this evening, I don't want you to be too envious. Someone had to show Andrea that she couldn't shoot the biggest deer."

"Must have gotten a nice one," George said.

"It's going to cost me money," Jim replied.

"Oh yeah? One of those?" questioned George.

"I'm afraid so," Jim replied. "It's right nice."

"Well, good for you!" Sam remarked. "I'm glad for you."

"Yep, I'm right pleased," Jim replied. "Over and out."

The girls heard Jim talking outside and opened the cabin door. "What's going on?" Andrea asked.

"Oh, not much," Jim answered humorously. "I just thought I'd take a little walk and get my Cherokee."

"What'd ya get?" Andrea asked.

"Well, we're deer huntin', so I'd say you could assume that I got a deer." Jim looked at her and grinned.

"Huh!" Andrea responded. She looked at her deer on the meat pole. "Think you could top that?"

Jim looked at her and laughed. "I'll let you be the judge of that after a while. I've got to go back out and get it so I can have it hanging up for the men to see when they get back." Jim walked into the cabin, put his gun in the gun rack, and threw his backpack into the corner of the room. "I could use some help loading it. It's that big." Andrea looked at Susan. "Well, shall we?" she asked.

"Why not?" Susan answered back.

The three went out to get into Jim's Cherokee. Andrea opened the passenger front door and motioned for Susan to get in. When Susan hesitated, Andrea said, "Oh, go ahead, Susan. Jump in!" Susan got in and shut the door and Andrea opened the back and jumped in.

Jim got in, looked over at Susan and grinned. "Some people think they know how to shoot big deer. Well, I think we're going to see who the big-chief deer hunter is." He laughed, looked at Susan again, and winked. "We're going to see who gets a run for their money on this one."

"Did you get a nice one?" Susan asked.

"Yup," said Jim with a grin. "I would say I got a right nice one."

"Oh, no!" Andrea said from the back seat. "That's okay, though, because I got the first one. I bet you didn't get an eight-pointer."

"You're right," Jim responded. "I just wasn't able to get an eight-pointer."

The women continued to ask Jim about his deer during the short drive back to Jim's deer stand. Jim just sat there smiling, shaking his head back and forth. When he reached the stand, he pulled up to the edge of the alfalfa field and stopped his Cherokee.

"I don't see a deer," Susan said after she had gotten out.

"No," Andrea said, "I don't see any deer either."

Jim turned and started walking into the woods. The women followed. All of a sudden, Jim heard Andrea gasp, "Oh, my!"

"What?" Susan asked.

"Look at it, Susan!"

"Where is it?"

"There!" Andrea pointed. "Look at the antlers sticking up! Oh, my!"

Jim continued to walk toward his deer. Finally, Susan saw the antlers sticking up. "Is that as big as yours, Andrea?"

"Is that as big as mine?" Andrea queried. "I believe cousin Jim outdid himself. My, what a deer!"

Jim squatted down and picked up the antlers in both hands. Somehow it seemed bigger than it had been when he had left it.

Susan stared. "I think you shot Bambi for sure!" she sighed.

Jim looked at her and grinned. "If it wasn't Bambi, it was his first cousin!"

Andrea laughed. "How many is it? Eight, nine, ten? A ten-pointer? I guess you didn't shoot an eight-pointer!" Andrea squatted down beside Jim and let her fingers touch each of the ten points, subconsciously counting each one again. "And look how wide! Jim, that is a deer and a half!"

"No, just one deer," said Jim, "but a mighty fine deer it is. I'm very grateful and very humbled to be able to have harvested such an animal."

"It is bigger than Andrea's, isn't it?" Susan asked.

"It's a big one. I'm going to put it in my den, in my study, at home."

"A deer in the house?" Susan asked. "It would be awful to have that thing looking at you."

"On the contrary, Susan," said Jim. "It will be wonderful to have it in my house. That way, I can see it every day to help me remember this afternoon for the rest of my life. It is a wonderful day, you know."

Susan looked at Jim and felt the heat rising from her neck to her ears. She wasn't exactly sure to what Jim was referring, but down deep inside she felt that it had been a wonderful day.

"Well, let's get it loaded," Jim said. "I want this deer hanging up. We need something to balance the other little runt that's hanging there."

"Runt, my eye!" Andrea retorted.

"Okay, I know, I know. There will be two good deer hanging on the meat pole," Jim laughed. "Let's get this thing pulled out to the jeep and get it loaded."

With the help of the two women, Jim was able to get the deer loaded and back to the cabin. Andrea went to get a stepladder while Jim went inside and got another ratchet rope. In short order they had the deer hanging up on the other side of the meat pole. "I think we need to get a picture of this," Jim smiled. "That's two good bucks hanging there. Let me get a picture of the two of you standing beside Andrea's deer."

The women obliged. Jim took several snapshots, and then positioned himself at an angle so he could take a snapshot of both deer on the pole.

"Here, Jim," Susan said. "Give me your camera and I'll take one of you next to your deer." Susan took the camera from him and snapped a picture with Jim's face in a big smile.

"Here, Susan," Andrea said. "Give me the camera and get in there beside Jim."

Susan turned to Andrea with a questioning look on her face. "I wasn't with him when he got his deer, like I was with you," Susan stated.

"That's all right," Andrea said. "Go on and stand beside Jim. We'll get a picture of him and his deer."

Jim felt the tops of his ears turning red. *Did she mean "deer" or "dear"?* he thought. He wasn't sure which Andrea meant, but he knew that both he and Susan were certainly aware of the connotation.

Andrea took the picture of Jim and Susan looking up at Jim's deer. "Now look at each other," Andrea chirped. Jim and Susan stared at Andrea for a moment and then looked at each other.

"I could look into those brown eyes all day long, Susan," Jim said.

Susan smiled. She could still feel the heat rising in her neck. Andrea took the picture, and the moment was broken.

"I wonder if I ought to take the stepladder back to the basement or if somebody else is going to come in with something this evening," Andrea said.

"Might as well leave it there for now," Jim replied. He went and found a stick the right length and separated the hind legs of his deer. It was thirty degrees outside, and the deer would chill well overnight and be preserved.

Jim heard another shot in the distance and took his bearings. Nope, it wasn't from George or Sam. It was nearing dusk, and he knew that the deer would be moving. It would be the perfect time to hunt. Jim smiled. This day, an hour earlier had been the perfect time for him to hunt.

Jim and the women went back into the cabin. "What's for supper tonight?" Jim asked.

"We have steak," said Andrea. "Do you want them broiled or grilled over the charcoal?"

"Broiled," Susan said.

"Grilled," Jim responded.

Andrea laughed. "Y'all are going to have to get your act together." Jim looked at Andrea and Susan and then shrugged and walked into the cabin. He went to the refrigerator and took out a slice of cheese to eat along with some tea. With his appetite, he couldn't wait for supper. He wanted something to nibble on.

Jim felt as though he was on cloud nine. This had been one of the best days of his life. Yet, he couldn't help wondering what Andrea had meant when she had referred to "his deer." He sneaked another slice of cheese and shook his head. He had to get a grip. He needed another day of hunting to help settle his nerves and give him some time to meditate and pray. He still had a doe tag, and he wondered if he should try to fill it in the morning. Sure, he would! Why not? That was why he was here!

It was another forty-five minutes before George and Sam drove into the lane. Again, the men piled out and made a beeline to the meat pole. "Oh, me!" George all but shouted. Sam looked and let out a grunt. "Jim, I told you that deer was mine! I had him all pegged. How in the world did you get him?"

"He walked up to me and said, 'shoot me,' so I shot him!" Jim teased. "Is that really the one you've been seeing?"

"If it isn't, then it's his twin brother!" Sam remarked. "That's one nice deer. How many points is it? Ten?"

"Yep," Jim said.

George looked at the deer. "Looks like you *will* be spending some money at the taxidermy shop this time around, won't you?"

"Afraid so," Jim answered.

The women came back out of the cabin. "Do you guys want your steaks broiled or grilled?" Andrea asked. "We've got a vote for each so far."

The overwhelming majority was for charcoal-grilled. Jim smiled. "Have you gotten it started yet?" he asked.

"Yes," Andrea laughed. "I already knew what the answer would be. The charcoal has been lit for twenty minutes. You guys get cleaned up. Did either of you two get anything?"

"No," Sam replied. "We're just a couple of weary hunters, without success, hungry as bears."

"Come in and clean up then. Who wants to cook the meat?" Andrea asked.

"I will," Jim replied.

"Can I help?" Susan asked.

"I guess about all the help I need is somebody to watch," Jim said. He looked into those toffee-toned eyes. The different shades of brown, interwoven together, mesmerized him to where he just couldn't keep from looking at them. Like a spider weaving a web, they were slowly weaving an enchantment around him that he couldn't shake. *You don't fall in love because of eyes,* he thought. He had to get a hold on himself.

"Sure, I'll watch," Susan said. "Unless they need me inside."

"We have the potatoes ready to mash and the carrots all but cooked," Martha responded. "Go ahead and help to make sure he doesn't burn the steaks. I want mine medium rare."

"Medium rare?" Susan shuddered. "That's like eating raw meat."

"No, not raw," Jim said. "Medium rare is a real pretty pink, a bright pink . . . there's nothing raw about that. It's the best way to eat a steak."

"I'll take mine well done, please," Susan said, giving Jim a skeptical look.

Jim looked at Susan and smiled. "Tell you what," he said. "How about if you go help out Martha and Andrea. I'll cook 'em, and you help eat 'em." George and Andrea looked at each other, shook their heads and walked into the cabin.

Fifteen minutes later, Jim brought in the steaks. "Ready for supper?" he asked. Martha, Andrea and Susan had mashed the potatoes and finished cooking the carrots, so they were ready to sit down around the table to eat their meal. Again, they held hands and they bowed their heads. Susan was sitting next to Jim, and this time she found comfort in the familiarity of holding his big hand in hers. George led the prayer of thanksgiving for a safe day, a successful day, and for the food. Then they began their meal.

"Here, Susan, here's your steak," Jim said. "I did yours longer than the rest. Close your eyes and eat it."

Susan took the steak and cut it. It was a dull pink inside. The color made her grimace, and she was tentative in taking the first bite. However, the more she chewed, the more she enjoyed the tenderness and the flavor that it held. "This is good," she confessed.

"Nah, it's still too well done," Jim said. "But at least you're learning,"

"I'm glad to eat it this way, but no more rare than this for the first time around," Susan replied.

The group ate the rest of their meal with a lot of excited talk. Jim had to tell the story of how he'd seen his buck and how he'd shot it.

"That thing must weigh at least 145 pounds and score 145 according to the Boone and Crocket scoring system," George said.

"I'd like to think so," Jim replied. "The tines are long, it's a ten-pointer, and it is an awfully pretty buck."

"Certainly worthy to be put on the wall," Sam said.

"I still can't believe that you would have an animal looking at you in your house," Susan said. "It just seems creepy."

Andrea looked at Susan. "There's a big difference between what people in the city and people in the country consider the norm," she said. "The only reason we don't have any deer heads in our house is that George hasn't, as yet, shot one big enough that he's wanted to have mounted."

"But that's going to change," George said in a huff.

Andrea laughed. "I hope so. We need a couple of good deer heads in our home." Susan just shook her head.

"This will be my second," said Jim. "Now I can balance the wall out in my den."

"Susan, you may not realize it, but we have a couple of deer heads in the cabin," Sam said.

"I haven't seen them," Susan replied.

"They're in our bedrooms," Martha said.

"You *sleep* with them?" Susan asked.

"No, I sleep in bed with my wife, and the deer stays on the wall," Sam replied. Everyone laughed. Susan shrugged and gave up. She continued to enjoy her steak, potatoes and carrots.

"Well, I guess tomorrow's another day," George said. "I think, though, that I'll go right back to where I was today. That has to be a good spot. I've killed deer there for the last three years. There are plenty of signs; I just haven't seen the right one yet."

"Yeah, well," said Sam, "I'm not sure what I'm going to do now. I was hunting that big buck, but I think Jim got him."

"Oh, there're more around, I'm sure," Jim said. "And anyway, we'll get to go again tomorrow." They finished their meal with some light chit-chat, and then the men did the dishes and the women sat down to watch a video.

George looked up. "What video is that?" he asked. "*Charlotte's Web* again? That's not a hunting video. This is a hunting cabin!"

"Yeah, but you men aren't watching the videos now, we are," Andrea said.

George shook his head. Of all movies to watch, how had they snuck that one into the cabin? The guys shrugged their shoulders, turned around and continued doing the dishes.

"I could help them," Susan offered, standing to her feet.

"No, you won't, Susan!" said Andrea. "You come over here and sit down and let those men work. We've done our share, and now it's time for them to do theirs. We still have a day and a half here. We're not going to spoil those men yet!" Susan gave a sideways glance at Jim and came and sat back down in the recliner. She closed her eyes and listened to *Charlotte's Web* while her mind took in the day's activities. Never had she experienced such a day as this.

"Hey, Susan," George said, interrupting her thoughts. "I've been wanting to ask you something. Where did you get that black eye?"

Susan involuntarily put her hand to her eyebrow. With all the events of the day, she had forgotten about her eye and how sore it was. "Black eye?" she asked.

"Oh, yes, very black!" George said. "Well, some black, some purple, some brown . . ."

Susan jumped up and headed to the bathroom to look in the mirror. When she saw her eye, she groaned. "I, uh . . . I guess I must have hit something," she said.

"Looks to me like Jim's cheek is kind of black and blue, too," Andrea said. Jim looked at Andrea, his eyes boring into her. Andrea ignored him. "Did you hit something in the woods, Jim?" Jim kept staring at Andrea while everyone else turned to look at Jim.

"Mercy, your cheek bone looks about the right height for an eyebrow," George quipped.

Jim didn't say a word. He went back to drying the dishes.

"Uh, Jim, we're waiting," Andrea said.

"I just can't see in the dark," Jim said. Everybody laughed. "I think I'll go get my doe in the morning," he continued, trying to get the attention off his black eyes and cheekbones. "I have a doe tag, and I would like to get me some doe meat to eat. I think I'll go to my other stand. It hasn't been disturbed, yet, this fall."

It grew quiet in the cabin after this, as each person pondered his or her own thoughts. The background hum of *Charlotte's Web* made soft lullaby sounds suitable for minds working, thinking and relaxing.

Jim finished drying the dishes and sat down on the sofa. He had an urge to get up and go out in the dark and look at his buck with a flashlight, but he knew he would take a ribbing about it if he did. He thought back over the afternoon and the buck stepping onto the trail before he had shot it. What a day it had been. He grinned and relaxed. It wouldn't be long before he could get everybody to bed for the evening and he could lie down on the couch and rest. Suddenly, he felt very tired. It had been a long day, but one filled with exhilaration. It had been a day of promise; a day to mark new beginnings.

"The Lord sure is good," Jim said out loud to no one in particular. Someone in the cabin picked up the refrain and said, "The Lord is good indeed."

"And it would also be good," Jim continued, "if you all would go to bed. That way I can go to bed."

"At 8:30 in the evening?" George remarked.

"It has been a long day," Jim said. "I'm tired."

"By the way," Martha interjected, "if anybody's curious, when I went out today to the store, I bought a nightlight for the bathroom. That way we won't have any freight train collisions tonight." It got quiet for a few seconds. Susan blushed again, feeling the heat rush up her neck to her ears.

Jim threw up his hands in disgust. "All right, I guess you're right. A little nightlight wouldn't hurt any of us." George, Sam, Andrea, and Martha looked at each other and laughed.

Gradually, each person stood, yawned, and went to their respective bedrooms. Jim got his sleeping bag from the corner of the room and laid it out on the couch. He adjusted his pillow, took off his clothes, and got into his sleeping bag. It had been a long day. Tomorrow wouldn't be what today was, but still, the chance to shoot a doe, to be in the woods, to observe the nature around him, to have some peace and quiet . . .

Jim prayed a prayer of thanks to God for being alive and for being able to enjoy life so abundantly. Then he drifted off to sleep.

Chapter 8

Jim, George, and Sam were up early the next morning, though not quite as early as the morning before. They didn't have the same adrenaline rush giving them the sense of urgency and adventure as they had had the morning before. Jim was in no hurry. With his ten-pointer "in the bag", it was almost anticlimactic to go out that morning, though he still looked forward to being in the woods.

They had a quick breakfast and slipped away from the cabin. The women had slept in. George turned and looked at Sam. "Well, it's our turn today, ol' boy," he said. "Let's do it!"

Sam smiled. He shined the flashlight over to the meat pole and looked at the deer hanging there. "A couple of mighty nice deer there," he said. "I'd like to add a couple more before the day is over."

"Let's go do it then, good buddy."

The men got into Sam's truck, and he drove each one of them to the deer stand where they wanted to sit that morning. Jim climbed into his stand and again settled down, waiting for the light to drive away the darkness. Since they were a little later this morning, Jim could already see the trees around him. The forest floor below him was just beginning to be visible.

Jim settled down and closed his eyes, letting his mind clear. He quickly nodded back to a light sleep. After several minutes had passed, his body suddenly jerked awake. He looked up. It was light. "Okay," he said, smiling to himself, "let's get some meat!"

Jim slowly rolled his eyes from side to side, letting his head swivel slightly as he surveyed the woods in front of him. To his surprise, he caught motion. A deer was coming out of the alfalfa field and heading back toward the thicket through the open woods. *I'll be the first one to shoot this morning,* he thought. He carefully raised his rifle and scoped the deer. A frown came across his face. *Oh, no,* he thought. *Normally I'm happy to see this, but not today.* It was a six-point buck, the rack fifteen inches wide. If it made it through this hunting season, it would make a nice trophy for next year. Jim had already killed his buck, and because each hunter could bag only one buck per season, he had no more tags to fill in Pennsylvania.

Too bad this isn't Virginia, he thought. *That deer would be mine.* Jim eased the rifle down, sat back and watched as the deer carefully meandered its way through the woods and back into the thicket.

Jim watched for more deer. A movement to his right caught his attention, and he saw a squirrel scurry from tree to tree, stopping to place an acorn into the ground where he would hide it for food for the winter. Jim marveled at the way God replenished the oak trees. The squirrels wouldn't find all of the acorns that they buried, and the acorns they buried would sprout and begin growing. Who knew? In eighty years, it could be a big, mature white oak tree.

Jim looked at his watch. It was the perfect time of morning. His mind drifted back home to the congregation that he served and to the families who were struggling with accepting someone they feared. How would the church cope? How would the community cope? Did they understand God's forgiveness? Would the people in the church and the community accept the fact that God can change lives? Or would their fear and distrust override their beliefs and make it difficult for Ernest to be a member of the community and worship with them?

As Jim sat there, he quietly prayed for his congregation. He prayed for his community and for Ernest, who would soon be out of prison. *There's so much evil in the world,* he thought. *Yet, by the grace of God, evil is conquered.*

Out of the blue, thoughts of Susan's striking eyes slammed into Jim's consciousness. A look of wonder spread across his face. What was it about Susan that was different? Yes, she had those multi-shaded brown eyes that he could look into forever, but there was something else about her—his being had never been stirred in such a way before. The more he was around Susan, the more he enjoyed being around her. Something about her turned his insides upside down and gave him a spark of excitement.

Jim wondered about her background, the stresses and the turmoil that she had been through. He wanted a family. Would that be something she could handle? Being in the center of the church and the community added extra pressure on his life, and it would only add pressure to hers. He felt as though he was under a microscope with everything that he did. If he wanted to know Susan better, it would be a delicate thing to accomplish. He wasn't sure how he should even handle pursuing a relationship with her. "Help me, God, to know how to pursue this relationship, if that is what You want," he prayed. "Give me Your direction and guidance."

He looked ten years into the future, daydreaming about what it would be like to wake up in the morning and be next to her. What would it be like to come home to her after a long, tiring, stressful day? Would he find peace and solace at home? Would he find a loving wife who cared for him and stood beside him? He certainly wasn't seeing anything at this point that marred that dream. Yet, he prayed again, "God, give me guidance. Help me to know Your will. Surely, Your will is where I'll find peace."

At that instant, Jim heard a noise in the leaves, and three deer came out of the alfalfa field at a dead run. Jim pulled his gun up and whistled, but the deer kept running. *There were some legal deer there, and they got past me without a shot,* he thought. *Oh, well.* He settled back down, but now he was more alert, watching and waiting for another deer to come out of the woods.

Back at the cabin, the women were enjoying fried eggs, sausage, toast and orange juice. "I believe I could learn to enjoy this," Susan said contentedly. "This is certainly the good life. I haven't felt so relaxed and at peace in a long, long time." She looked at Andrea. "I'm so grateful that you and George let me come along."

"It certainly has worked out well, and we have enjoyed having you here. Besides, you've gotten to see what life is like outside of the city limits. You've been able to get a glimpse of what it's like to enjoy the great outdoors."

And, Susan thought, *to meet a man who is really intriguing.*

Martha looked at Susan. "Your black eye doesn't look quite as bad today as it did yesterday. But I don't think that we can let Jim off the hook too easily."

"What do you mean?" Susan questioned.

Martha looked at Andrea. "I think we need to doctor that up some," she said.

"Doctor it?" Susan asked. She put her fingers to her eyebrow. It was still sore, but the swelling had gone down. Susan jumped up, went to the bathroom and looked in the mirror. She definitely had a black eye, but it was more yellow today. It was starting to spread out as the blood began to diffuse back into her body.

Andrea looked at Martha. "You know, you're right," she said. "We can't let Jim off the hook this easily. We have to make sure he's been adequately punished for his night walking."

Susan returned to the table, listening to the conversation. *Now, what do they have in mind?* she thought.

"Let's finish breakfast," Andrea said. "Martha, what kind of makeup do you have in your pocketbook?"

"Exactly the right stuff," Martha replied.

Susan looked at them. "What do you two have in mind?"

Martha jumped up to grab her purse. "It seems to me like that black eye is starting to fade out," she said. "We need to make it more pronounced. It needs to look bad when those men come back."

Susan put her hand over her mouth. "Oh, no!"

"Oh, yes!"

The women finished their breakfast and did the dishes, giggling over how the men would react. "We didn't get up until after the men left to hunt, so they haven't seen you this morning. But they'll certainly see you at lunch time."

"Okay, Susan, come on!" said Andrea. "We're going to fix you up just fine." Susan tentatively walked over to the chair and sat down.

"What all do you have?" she asked.

Martha emptied her purse. Andrea perused the contents and pulled out some eye shadow, blush and eyeliner. "Oh boy, we'll get him this time," she said to Martha. "We'll get Jim for sure."

"What do you mean?" Susan was hesitant.

"You just watch. We'll take care of him. Hold still, Susan." Andrea began to gently apply makeup to Susan's eye.

"What are you doing?" Martha exclaimed. "You're covering up the black eye instead of making it worse."

"Well, now, you don't think that Susan can have two black eyes, do you?"

"What do you mean, two black eyes?" Susan didn't understand.

"Well, you'll only have one black eye," but it's going to be your other eye that's black today when the guys come in."

Martha roared. "Oh, this will be good!"

Susan sat there feeling a bit apprehensive. A part of her was laughing at playing a trick on Jim, but another part of her was wondering what his reaction would be.

"Do you want to find out what kind of man Jim is?" asked Andrea. "Well, this is one way to find out. This is going to be good."

Susan grinned. "Okay, go for it.

Andrea took the eye shadow, coloring the eye that was perfectly good to give Susan a huge black eye. They worked over her for fifteen minutes and then stood back with their hands on their hips and looked at their creation with satisfaction. "Absolutely stunning!" Martha said. "They won't be able to miss this."

Susan jumped up and ran to the bathroom to look in the mirror. "Oh, my!" she said. "Oh, my . . . are you sure this is a good idea?"

"Jim needs to be trimmed," said Andrea. "After he got that big buck yesterday, we'll get him. We can't let him get away with being the king on the hill. We'll take him down a few notches."

"Okay, I guess we'll see how he reacts," Susan agreed, grinning.

Martha began to put her makeup away. "I need to go back to my house and take care of a few things," she said. "You two be good while I'm gone. I'll be back for lunch to see how the fellows react."

After Martha left, Susan again went to the bathroom to look at her eye. She shook her head in wonderment. How much ribbing could Jim take? Well, she would certainly like to know him better, and she believed she was about to learn a little more about him.

Five minutes after Martha left, the women heard a vehicle approaching in the driveway. "I wonder what Martha forgot?" Andrea asked. She looked out. "Oh, it's not Martha, it's George! That could only mean one thing. Come on, Susan. George must have gotten his deer."

The women walked down the steps of the cabin and over to the vehicle. George was already out and back by the tailgate. He was grinning. "I may not have gotten one as big as Jim, or you, my dear, but it's a legal buck, and I'm happy to get it."

Susan and Andrea crowded around, peering into the back of Sam's truck. It was a seven-pointer with a fourteen-inch spread. "Most likely a two-and-a-half year old deer," George commented. "It will be perfect for eating."

Susan looked at George's deer and then at the other deer that had already been hung up. "I'll get the ladder." She marveled at how she was fitting into this whole new way of life.

"I'll help you," said Andrea.

They got the ladder from the basement, and George got a rope. It didn't take long to have the deer hanging and washed out. "Three on the meat pole," he said. "Three bucks. That's a good year. And we still have Sam to go. I heard someone shoot, and I think that the shots came from the direction where he hunts. I hope he was able to get his deer."

"And now that Jim has gotten his big one, he can only shoot a doe. Is that right?" asked Susan.

"That's right," Andrea replied.

"It seems like that would be a letdown after shooting such a beautiful deer." Susan again looked at the ten-pointer. She marveled at the sheer beauty of the animal.

"Jim likes to hunt, and, yes, he killed the deer of a lifetime," said Andrea. "But he also enjoys being out in the peace and quiet of the woods, and he will enjoy shooting a doe."

"I need to go back out at 11:30 to pick up Sam and Jim," George said. "But first, I'm going to come in and have a snack and see what you gals are fixing for lunch."

When Susan looked at George, he did a double take. Her eye looked horrible! He wondered what he should say. How sensitive was she? "It looks like Jim must have walloped you pretty good . . ." he said. "That eye looks bad."

"Oh, it's feeling terrible this morning," Susan replied.

George heard a snicker. He turned to his wife with a questioning look, and then back to Susan. "What's going on here?" he asked.

"Oh, I've got a bad eye this morning," Susan explained.

George shook his head and walked into the cabin. He pulled out a block of Muenster cheese, cut off a slab and got out the crackers. He would wash it all down with a soft drink. He saw the women look at each other and heard a stifled giggle. Something wasn't right. When he looked at Susan again, she involuntarily put her hand to her sore eye. *That's it,* George realized. He stared at Susan, and with a straight face said, "It looks as if you've had another run-in. Who gave you a black eye this morning? I don't believe Jim gave you that one." He looked at Andrea. He knew his wife well enough to know that there was mischief in the air. "Who came up with this brilliant idea?"

"What brilliant idea?" Andrea said innocently.

"I'll bet you could take some soap and water and clean that black eye off pretty easily," George replied.

Andrea and Susan both laughed. "Okay, okay. You're pretty observant, but how observant will Jim be?"

George laughed along with them. "Well, we'll make it as hard on him as we can." He finished his cheese and crackers, downed the rest of his soda and walked back out to where his prize was hanging to take a couple of pictures. "I hope Sam gets his deer. I'd sure like to get a picture of four bucks on that pole all at one time. We need to get these deer skinned. We've had a good hunt, but we're going to need to take care of the meat."

"What do you do with the deer now?" Susan asked.

"We'll skin them out. It's been cold enough that the meat has not spoiled. Jim will get his deer head mounted."

Andrea looked at George. "It seems to me that there's another deer up there that could be mounted," she suggested.

George looked at Andrea for a moment until he comprehended what she was saying. For his wife's first deer, that was a mighty nice animal. It would mean a lot to her to have it hanging in their home where she could brag about it and how she had pulled a fast one on the men. "I guess I could come up with a couple hundred bucks," George drawled in a slow voice. "That should pay half of what it will cost to get your deer mounted. Do you know of anybody who could come up with the other 50 percent?"

Andrea looked at him. "Could we?"

"You bet," George said. "Then you could put it wherever you want to in the house."

Andrea was thrilled. She hadn't really thought about getting her buck mounted, but it was a nice deer—and it was her first. She would always be able to remember how she had put one over on the men whenever she looked at the deer. "I believe I know someone who could come up with the other 50 percent," she said. "George, you are the sweetest man I know."

George strutted around, hands on his hips, and began to sing:

I'm the sweetest man that ever was,
But a close second may be your 'cuz.'

We'll mount yours and he'll mount his;
We'll remember this year for what it is.

"And what is it?" asked Susan.

"It's the year that a lot of big boys bit the dust," said George, "and not only four-legged deer, but other big boys as well."

Susan's ears began to burn red. "Shame on you, George," Andrea scolded. She looked at Susan. "We just don't know what all may come of this year, do we?"

Susan looked at her friend and her husband. "You people are impossible!"

"Oh, we may be impossible," George laughed, "but we sure are having fun."

Andrea walked over to where Susan was standing and put an arm around her. "Susan, we're glad that you're here. We don't know all the ways that the good Lord works, and we don't know the outcome or what the future may hold, but we certainly have had a good time and we're glad that you're a part of it. As far as a relationship is concerned, we'll let things take their course." She turned back to George. "Shame on you, George, for picking on her so much!"

"Me, picking on her? I'm just telling the truth." Andrea threw a rag at him. He ducked and ran back inside.

"I think we'd better start getting lunch together," Susan said, trying to change the subject. "What are we going to fix today?"

"I don't know," Andrea replied. She walked over to the kitchen counter and looked at the menu. "It looks like today we're supposed to eat whatever leftovers we have, plus toasted cheese sandwiches."

"That sounds good," Susan replied. "We have plenty of time to get lunch ready."

George sneaked back into the cabin, turned on a hunting video and sat down on the recliner. "This is certainly a rough life," he said.

The women looked at George and shook their heads.

Andrea put her finger to her lips and quietly went to the sink. She drew a dozen drops of water into a glass and handed it to Susan. Susan looked at Andrea with a puzzled look on her face. Andrea motioned for her to go over and dump the water on George. Susan shook her head, but Andrea motioned with her hands for her to go on, so Susan quietly walked over to George and leaned over the recliner. She put the glass six inches above George's face and turned it over ever so slowly, allowing a couple of drops to splash on his face. George's reaction was immediate. His arms came up, and he grabbed and got hold of Susan and pulled her down to him. Susan squealed and Andrea laughed.

George opened his eyes. "Whoops! Wrong woman. My wife put you up to that." George released Susan, jumped out of the chair and headed for Andrea. Andrea shrieked and took off outside. George flew out the door and chased her around the cabin.

Susan stood in the doorway as Andrea came around the cabin with George hot on her heels. He caught her in front of the cabin by the meat pole, planted a solid kiss on her lips and held her tight. Something stirred within Susan. The relationship she had had with her husband had been good, but she didn't remember any of the fun and spontaneity that she saw displayed in front of her. She wondered what it would be like to have Jim hold her and kiss her that way. She shook herself. *Jim would never want me,* she thought. *He's a minister, and I've had a couple of rough years – rough years when I've had to take medication for my depression. If he's a minister, he needs a wife who is solid and stable.*

George looked at his watch. "I'm going to go out and get Sam. I hope he has his deer so we'll have a grand slam on the pole."

"Don't forget Jim," Susan reminded.

"Oh, I could never forget him," George replied. "Of course, you could take his Cherokee out to pick him up."

"Oh, no," Susan said, "you're not doing that."

George laughed and jumped into Sam's truck. He backed his way around the other vehicles and started down the lane to pick up Sam and Jim. The women walked back into the cabin. They were both charged with electricity and vivacity.

"It's good to be alive, isn't it, Susan?" Andrea remarked. "You need a good man to grab you and hold you . . . besides George."

Susan laughed. "I'm glad you got the punishment from him instead of me! But yes, you're right. I do miss being held."

"That will change for you someday . . . maybe sooner than later." Andrea looked at Susan and winked.

Susan shrugged. "One never knows."

The women started to prepare lunch in anticipation of the men's return. When they heard a vehicle in the driveway, Susan ran over to see who it was.

"It's just Martha," she called over her shoulder.

"Oh, you're looking for the men, are you?" Andrea said, her eyes twinkling.

Susan blushed. "Well, I want to see if they've gotten more deer."

Andrea grinned. "We'll know soon."

Right after she said that, they again heard the sound of a vehicle. Susan looked out and said, "Here they are!" The women opened the door and walked out onto the porch. The men piled out of Sam's truck.

"What'd you get?" Andrea asked.

"Meat," was the response.

"Let's go see what kind of little deer these guys got," Andrea said to Susan.

They all gathered around the back of the truck. There lay a six-pointer. It might have been the smallest of the lot, but Sam didn't care. He had completed the grand slam—four tags and four bucks.

"We're liable not to have any good bucks left on this place for next year," George said.

"At least I know where there's one good buck for next year," Jim said.

"There are plenty of deer," Sam replied. "I saw several smaller bucks that weren't legal. Give them a year or two, and they'll be there. There were six others with this one, and they were running a doe. This was the one I was able to get."

"How about you, Jim?" Susan asked. "Where is your doe?"

"I didn't get her," Jim replied. "She flew by me so quickly I never had a chance to get a shot off."

"I guess I'll have to show you how," Susan teased. Jim looked at her. Instantly, realizing what she had said, Susan felt her ears getting red. "Well, I did go with Andrea when she got hers," she added timidly.

Jim smiled. "That may be a good idea. This afternoon, I'll let you show me where they are."

The men got the deer hung up and washed out in no time. Andrea went into the cabin and brought out several cameras to take pictures. "The good Lord has certainly blessed us with a full meat pole this year," she said. They all stood and gazed at the deer.

"Well, look at it now, fellas," Jim said. "I'm going to cape my deer out this afternoon before I go back out so I can get it mounted. I need to get the hide off, because tomorrow we need to take them to the butcher shop."

Sam looked at the deer. "Yes, I'd rather take it to the butcher shop than try to cut it up myself, though I will take the tenderloins out."

Jim turned to walk away. "What's for lunch?" he asked.

"Leftovers and grilled cheese sandwiches," Andrea replied. "But the leftovers are pretty thin. You guys might starve until supper time."

"Not me," Jim said. "Somebody start up the grill. I'll skin my buck right now, and we'll have tenderloin on the grill to go along with those sandwiches."

"That old deer will be so tough, it won't taste good at all," George said.

"We'll find out," Jim challenged.

The women went back into the cabin. Sam started the charcoal, and the other two men lowered Jim's deer so they could skin it out. "Let's make sure we cut the cape back far enough so as to give the taxidermist plenty of hide to work with," Jim said. In short order they had skinned the deer and lifted the backstraps out. They took them into the cabin and laid them on the counter to butterfly them.

"That will make some good eating," Andrea said.

Susan walked over and looked at the meat. "You're supposed to eat that?" she asked.

"No, you don't need to," Jim offered. Suddenly, he looked at Susan and stared. "You look pretty bad this morning."

"Yeah, it looks pretty bad," she said matter-of-factly.

Everyone came together to look at Susan's face. "Yes, I didn't want to say anything," Sam remarked, "but that eye does look pretty bad."

Andrea jumped into the conversation. "It seems to me that people ought to watch where they walk at night. I sure am glad that Martha got that night light."

Jim threw his hands up in the air. "I give, I give! I certainly didn't mean to collide with our guest in our cabin. Your eye does look bad, Susan. Does it feel okay?"

Involuntarily, Susan put her hand to the eye that hurt. Realizing her mistake, she quickly put it to the other eye. "Oh, it doesn't hurt as bad as it did," she said.

"You guys get these tenderloins grilled," said Andrea. "The sandwiches are almost done." She wanted to cut the conversation short so she could play on Jim's mind a little longer.

Jim shook his head. "I'm sorry," he said.

Susan looked at Jim and smiled. "Your cheek looks like it's starting to get better, Jim. It's one of those things that we'll remember from this trip for a long, long time."

"Yes, I guess you're right," Jim said. He looked again at the black eye on Susan's face. It looked awful, but he had a nagging thought that something wasn't quite right. He looked down from her black eyebrow and drank in the mysterious, different colors of her brown eyes.

Susan playfully gave him a push. "Oh, go on, Jim. We'll live. We're going to survive."

Jim turned and went outside to check on the tenderloins. Deer meat was one of his favorites, and tenderloin on the grill was absolutely the best! He felt that it changed flavor five minutes after he cooked it, so he always liked to eat a piece right off the grill. With deer meat being so lean and fat being what held the heat, Jim was able to take a piece of tenderloin and eat it while it was still good and hot.

"That's pretty good eating for a buck that age," he said after taking a bite. "Not bad. Not bad at all."

The guys finished grilling and took the meat inside. As they sat down around the table and held hands, Andrea interjected, "It's my turn to pray." Everyone looked at her as she bowed her head and began to pray. "Thank You, Father, for deer and for meat. Thank You for the fun and the fellowship. And thank You for black eyes. Amen."

Laughter erupted. Jim muttered, "You just won't let it alone, will you?" He looked over at Susan's black eye, and she returned the glance. George and Andrea snickered. "Pass the meat and the sandwiches, please," Jim said, trying to draw attention away from himself.

Something was still nagging at his mind. He looked back at Susan. "Tell me again how badly that eye hurts, Susan." Again, Susan put her finger to her sore eye and then quickly to the other eye. Like a flash, the light bulb went off in Jim's mind. "Excuse me a minute," he said. He got up, went to the bathroom, ran some water until it was warm, wet a washcloth, wrung it out and stoically walked back to the table. "Let me see your face," he said to Susan when he had returned. Susan leaned toward him so he could have a better look. "I promise not to kiss you. Just close your eyes so I'm not distracted." Susan obeyed, and Jim quickly brought the washrag up and took a swipe underneath her eye. A lot of the makeup came off on the washrag. "Just as I thought," Jim muttered.

Susan jumped back after feeling the wet washrag and opened her eyes. "How much does your eye hurt now?" Jim said. Laughter erupted as Sam sat there wondering what in the world was going on. He was the only one now who was outside the joke.

"Some black eye," Jim said. "Some black eye, indeed. Give me my toasted cheese sandwich." He looked over at Andrea. "You concocted that. You will never let it rest, will you?"

Andrea was laughing so hard that tears were streaming down her face. Jim looked at her. "That's okay. I'll forgive you. Black eye indeed."

They finished their lunch and George stretched. "I guess I'll go and skin my buck."

"I guess I will, too," the other guys said in unison.

"George, who's going to skin out Andrea's deer?" Jim asked. "If she's woman enough to shoot one, she ought to be woman enough to skin it out."

Andrea grunted. "We've got dishes to do."

"You didn't have dishes to do when you shot it," Jim remarked.

The guys put on their coats and went outside. George lowered his deer all the way to the ground and cut off its back legs below where bone and cartilage meet. He put slits in the skin between the bone and cartilage so he could put the ratchet ropes hooks through them, and hoist it up. He began skinning it from the rear, forward. He skinned it halfway, then raised it farther up on the meat pole, and continued to skin.

"It sure is a nice specimen," George commented. He repeated the process for Andrea's deer.

Sam looked at his buck. It was still a little warm from being bagged only several hours earlier. "Well, I might as well skin it out. It's easier to do while it's still warm."

The women finished the dishes and came out of the cabin to watch the men finish the skinning procedure. Susan wrinkled her nose as she took in the whole operation. This was so foreign to her, and she felt a touch of sadness and disgust at what she was seeing. She voiced her displeasure at the poor deer legs that lay on the ground.

"Just remember," Jim said, "when you get beef at the grocery store, that hamburger was once beef on the hoof, and it, too, made the ultimate sacrifice for you. It's the way of life."

"I know, I know," Susan came back. "It just seems so sad to have such a beautiful animal destroyed."

"Not destroyed," Jim said kindly. "Harvested. And it will make a lot of good eating for us."

Chapter 9

The men finished their task and pulled the deer back up to the top of the meat pole. Jim looked at his watch. It was three o'clock; high time for him to get back out to his tree stand if he wanted a chance at getting a doe that evening. "I think I'll go back to the same place," Jim said. "I'm still seeing deer there every time I hunt. I just wasn't able to get a shot at that doe this morning."

"I should go along and show you how," Susan offered quietly.

"You should what?" Jim squawked, forgetting his acceptance of her earlier offer.

"I helped Andrea get hers, didn't I? I went along and watched."

Jim pondered for a minute. Normally, he would be in a tree stand, but he could sit on the ground this evening. It wasn't as critical, he felt, for killing a doe as it would be for a buck. "I guess that would be fine. If you want to come along, you can." Inside, he was thrilled with the idea of Susan wanting to go along with him. "If you can help bring me a doe as nice as the buck you brought Andrea, then you're mighty welcome."

"I'll need to get bundled up. It's going to be pretty cold this evening."

"And you'll need to sit still, too. You can't be jumping around."

"Okay, I'll put on plenty of wrap so I can be still."

Andrea glanced over at George. The more she thought about it, the more pleased she was to see the relationship that was building between Susan and Jim. Susan was a good person. The last few years had been hard, and what she needed most was a new start to get away from past memories that haunted her. She would be the type of mate in whom Jim could revel—serious, yet fun-loving, easygoing, a good cook, someone who cared for and loved people.

Jim cleaned his hunting knife and put it in its sheath. "I need to get my wrap and my gun and a couple of cushions. We'll sit on the ground. I guess we'll take my Jeep so that Sam can go where he wants." Jim quickly got what he needed as Susan went inside to ask Andrea what she should wear.

Andrea helped Susan with a backpack that would carry extra wrap. "Don't put it all on now," she suggested. "Wait until you get to the stand. Otherwise, you'll work up a sweat as you walk in and then get a chill once you arrive."

Jim and Susan climbed into the Jeep Cherokee and started toward Jim's stand. "I hope you enjoy this," Jim said. "It's a very special spot that I take pleasure in year after year. It has almost always produced deer for me, and the peace and the quiet and the tranquility that I find sitting in the woods is something that I cherish."

"I understand," Susan replied cheerfully. "I think I will like it just fine."

Jim stopped his Jeep several hundred yards from where they were going. Quietly, he and Susan sneaked down to the edge of the woods toward the stand. Jim knew that by moving thirty yards to the right of the tree stand, they would have an elevated view from the ground, where they could easily see the deer trails and wooded thickets. "The deer should be coming out in the evening, heading for the alfalfa field," he explained to Susan. "During the day they lie up in the thickets for cover and then come out into the field in the evening to feed."

"This is going to be exciting," Susan whispered. "I never in all of my life dreamed that I would be deer hunting."

Jim quietly put the two cushions on the ground and pushed the leaves away so they could move their legs without making any noise. "Here are some earplugs," he said. "With these in your ears, the rifle crack won't be so loud and shocking to you if or when I shoot."

They sat side by side and lapsed into silence. A couple of squirrels played up and down the tree in front of them. They continued to sit. Jim's left hand fell down to his side. He sat there with his eyes closed, a sense of peace and contentment flooding over him as he allowed his ears to be his eyes. He was sure he would hear a deer if came out of the brush.

Susan sat there and slowly moved her head to the right to look at Jim. His eyes were closed. She looked at his hand lying there. It was so big, so masculine. She wanted to reach out and touch it, but didn't know if she dared. She continued to watch the squirrels. Without warning, the woods behind her rang with the drumming of a red-headed flicker. Susan involuntarily jumped. Jim never moved or opened his eyes. He just sat there quietly.

Susan couldn't believe how totally in tune with the woods they were. As they sat there, it seemed as if they were a part of it. She listened to the woods around them. What a difference it was from the city and the life that she had been living. Without thinking, Susan reached down and picked up Jim's hand. He didn't resist. She looked at his knuckles and his fingernails. She had gloves on and her hands were chilled, yet Jim wore none at all. She wondered how he could brave the cold.

Carefully, so as not to create a motion, Susan lifted Jim's hand higher and studied it. What would it be like for this hand to be her hand to hold and no one else's? Suddenly, on an impulse, she brought his hand up and laid a light kiss on the back of it. Jim's eyes opened. His head started to turn, but then went back to where it was. He closed his eyes again. Susan felt self-conscious of what she had done and slowly placed his hand back at his side.

An hour or more passed. Susan was becoming chilled, even though she had on an extra layer. Despite the cold, she still couldn't believe the sense of peace and contentment that she felt. She stole another look at Jim. His eyes were closed. However, she noticed that occasionally he would open them, carefully scan the area, and then close them again. So this was what it was like for him to hunt.

Susan looked up at him again and then toward the thicket. Instantly, she froze. There were three deer coming out into the clearing. She glanced at Jim. His eyes were still closed. She had seen them before he had. What should she do? She watched for another ten to fifteen seconds. The deer would advance a couple of steps and then stop, twitch their tails and hold their heads up, looking for possible danger.

When the deer put their heads down and started to walk again, Susan could no longer contain herself. She carefully put her arm between her and Jim and bumped him. "Deer!" she hissed. Jim's eyes opened and he immediately saw the deer. The deer stopped, their heads erect. Time stood still for Susan. What was Jim going to do? Why wasn't he doing something?

The deer began to walk forward and Jim, very slowly, began to raise his rifle. When they stopped again, Jim continued to quietly raise the rifle to his shoulder. He peered through the scope and placed the crosshairs right behind the front shoulder of one of the deer. Jim took a deep breath, exhaled and began to squeeze the trigger. The rifle cracked, and the deer jumped. The doe's hind legs kicked back behind her as she took off on a half arc heading back toward the thicket.

Jim looked around at Susan and grinned. "Good job," he said. "You did help me to get my deer."

"They were beautiful, Jim. Did you see all of them?"

"Well, yes, I saw them. I hit the biggest doe in the group."

"Can we go and get it now?"

"Let's wait a little while," Jim replied. "I believe you're more excited than I am!"

Susan's teeth started to chatter. The cold that had gradually chilled her, along with her emotions, made her body shake all over. Jim looked at her and laughed quietly. "You're a bundle of nerves."

"I'm so excited, Jim, I can hardly stand it," Susan replied. "I've been here only two days, and have watched both you and Andrea shoot a deer. This is so exciting."

"A few days ago you thought it was terrible."

"That was before I knew better." Susan looked at him and smiled.

Jim laughed. "Let's go get my doe."

They got up, and Susan took the earplugs out of her ears. "You're right; that rifle was loud, even with the earplugs."

They walked fifty yards to the edge of the woods where the deer had run back into the thicket. As they neared the spot, Jim glanced down and saw a blood trail on the ground. He stopped on the edge of the thicket and looked ahead. Just inside, only eight or nine yards in, lay his deer. "It looks like we'll have another skinning job in the morning," he said. "I'll have to let you help me skin this one, Susan, since you helped me shoot it."

Susan squirmed. "I guess if I'm going to be a country girl, I need to learn how to be one."

Jim grinned. He was enjoying spending time with Susan, and the future was definitely looking rosy and bright for him. But then he thought about his congregation and the struggles they would soon be going through. *It's good to have bright spots during the trials,* he thought. In that instant, Jim realized that while the hunting trip would soon be over, his relationship with the woman who stood beside him was one that needed to be cultivated. He shook his head and snapped back to the present. "Hold my rifle, and I'll go in and pull the deer out."

Susan took the rifle. It was the first one that she had ever held. "You'll have to show me what this rifle is all about," she said, "because I'm really afraid of it."

"It's actually good to be afraid of it," Jim replied, "because it is not a toy. But there's nothing to be afraid of if you treat it like a weapon." Jim pulled the doe around and made quick work of field dressing her. He got a rope out of his backpack and, together, he and Susan dragged the deer back to where they had been sitting. Jim got the rest of their gear packed up, and then they dragged the deer out to the alfalfa field. "Let's go get my Jeep," he said to Susan. "I can back it down along the alfalfa, and we won't have to drag it any farther than this."

The sun was casting long shadows across the yard when Jim and Susan drove up to the cabin. Andrea peered through the window as they piled out of the Jeep. *It looks like we have more meat,* she said to herself. She slipped on a coat and went outside. "I guess we might as well go and get the ladder," she said to Susan.

"That's right," Susan beamed. "I had to help get Jim another deer. He couldn't have done it without me."

Jim looked at her and guffawed. "I will admit that you did see it first," he said.

Susan went and helped Andrea. In her exuberance, she tried to tell Andrea everything that had happened all at once. As Andrea listened, she had a warm glow inside. She could see that this budding relationship could be good for Susan and Jim.

Susan and Andrea took the ladder to the meat pole. Jim got the ratchet rope, and they soon had the deer hanging. Five deer made for a full pole.

Everyone was in a festive mood around the supper table that evening. The steaks, the mashed potatoes and gravy and the salad had never tasted as good to Susan as it had this evening. Her cheeks were rosy from the cold, and now her black eye wasn't so black after being washed from her face. With all the excitement of the hunt and being close to Jim, she felt as though she were in a world of make-believe. It was a thrilling world for her, and she didn't want it to end.

They were a noisy crowd that evening as they chitchatted with each other and joked and ate. At one point, George looked over at Susan. "So you had to kill it for him, huh?" he said. "He wasn't able to do it himself?"

"He was trying to sleep," Susan replied. "He hardly opened his eyes the entire time."

Jim grinned. "I can see with my eyes closed."

"You can see all right. I had to punch you to let you know that those deer were there."

"Were you there to punch me when I got the big boy?"

"Well, I guess not. But you would have let those deer walk right past you!"

"I seriously doubt it. I bet they wouldn't have gone another fifteen to twenty feet before I would have seen them."

"Hmm! It was a good thing I was there."

Jim didn't have anything more to say. What could he say? "It looks as if we made a good pair getting that doe. Maybe we should keep working at being a pair."

Again, Susan started to turn red. Jim had been well aware of Susan's kiss on the back of his hand and how she had held his hand, and there wasn't anything about it that he didn't like. He was paving the way for Susan to know that he was not afraid of building a relationship.

Sam, Martha, George and Andrea all laughed. "It looks like this is not going to be a hunting camp anymore. It's going to be a matchmaking camp."

"Oh, cut it out!" Susan said. "I just had to help him a little bit, that's all."

Jim looked at them and grinned. "Yeah, I just needed a little help, that's all."

The men got up from the table and did the dishes. However, before the women could turn on the television, George sneaked over and put in a hunting video. The women groaned. "Oh, me. Now you're trying to have your cake and eat it too," George said. "This is a hunting cabin."

"Yeah, this isn't *Charlotte's Web* country," Jim added. "We've got hunting on our brains."

"You can say that again," George said. "Jim's really got hunting on his brain."

Jim threw a tea towel at him. George laughed and ducked, and then picked up the tea towel to return it to the kitchen. "Keep hunting, ol' boy," he whispered to Jim. "Keep hunting."

Chapter 10

The next morning, the guys slept in later than normal and didn't get up until around 7:30. While they were eating breakfast together, Jim, stretching, said, "I need to skin out that doe right quick. Then, I guess, we might as well pack everything up and head for Virginia."

"If you hadn't killed that doe, you wouldn't have to skin it," Andrea commented.

"If I hadn't killed that doe, I wouldn't have good meat to eat, either," Jim retorted. "That big boy I'll make into bologna and deer jerky. The doe I'll make into steaks, chops and burger."

"You're right," Andrea commented. "We do enjoy deer meat."

It took them a couple of hours to get all of the work done, tidy up the cabin and pack the Cherokee. The men threw a tarp up over the carrier rack on the jeep and laid the deer on top, covering them with the ends of the tarp. Then they tied the deer down tightly with plenty of rope so they could safely make the haul home.

They were a happy foursome as they headed back to Virginia. After driving for about an hour, Jim said, "It looks to me as if it's time for some gas. Do you all want to eat now, or do you want to wait until we're farther down the road?" He looked at his watch. It was only 11:30.

"Let's wait a little while," Andrea said. "We had a big breakfast, though I could use the restroom and a drink."

Jim pulled into a gas station and convenience store. He filled the tank with gas while the women went inside to get a drink. When Jim went to pay for his gas, the attendant looked at him and said, "You're on pump six?"

"That's correct," Jim said, "It's $34.50."

"It's already been paid for," the attendant responded.

"What do you mean, 'paid for'?" Jim asked. "I just got it."

"It's been paid for." The attendant looked at him, winked and nodded his head toward the women, who, by that time, were buying soft drinks.

Jim looked, shook his head and smiled. "Thanks," he said to the attendant.

Jim walked over to buy a drink. "What's going on, ladies? Who's the wise one?"

"What do you mean, 'wise one'?" Andrea said.

"You know what I mean," Jim said. "Who paid for my gas?"

Susan smiled. "That's a small down payment for the vacation you all have given me over the past couple of days. It's the least I could do."

Jim wasn't sure what to say or how to respond. Finally, a smile broke out on his face and he simply said, "Thanks. It was our pleasure."

They drove for another hour and a half before reaching Virginia. "Let's stop at a good restaurant," George suggested. They all agreed.

The four of them had an enjoyable lunch and were soon back on the road. After another hour and a half, they would be home. As they went to get back into the Cherokee, George and Andrea climbed into the back, forcing Susan to sit up front with Jim. "I need to sit in the back so I can hold Andrea's hand," George said.

Susan blushed as she remembered holding Jim's hand in the woods. Had Jim said anything to them? She would hardly think so. She glanced at Jim out of the corner of her eye. He never let on or said a word.

The time flew by quickly, and soon Jim was pulling into George and Andrea's driveway. "Now the work really begins," he said. "All the unpacking and putting everything away. I'll carry the deer over to the meat processing plant later this afternoon."

They unloaded all the gear, and the time came for Jim to leave. He grasped George's hand, shook it, and then gave him a bear hug. "Thanks, old buddy, for marrying my favorite cousin. You're a pal, and I love you to death."

"Return dittoes," George responded. "You certainly are a wonderful friend."

Jim hugged Andrea next. "Thank you, favorite cousin, for marrying George and for all the work you did to give us a good time. I appreciate you so much and love who you are and what you do."

"You have one more hug to give," Andrea whispered. Jim gave her a wicked look. As they separated, Andrea said in a more audible voice, "Jim you're the greatest. Thank you for being such a wonderful cousin as well."

Jim looked at Susan. It would be awkward not to give her a hug, and he found that he wanted to do so anyway. So he stepped forward and said, "Here, let me give you a hug, too. Thank you for crashing our party."

Susan responded to the hug with a squeeze. "Thank you for being patient and for letting me crash your party. You have been extremely kind, and I thank you for it."

Jim got into his Cherokee and drove to the butcher shop, then drove home to unpack and clean up. His mind was in the clouds. What a couple of days he had experienced! All the way home, his mind kept going over the harvest of his beautiful ten-pointer, his doe, and the fun of their hunting camp. He kept thinking about the time he had spent with Susan—how she had held his hand and kissed it—and about the hug when they had parted. Susan had shaken him more than any other woman had ever shaken him before. Something about her just made him want to be with her.

Suddenly, he stopped the car. He didn't even know Susan's address or her phone number. He hadn't made any inquiry as to how he could get in touch with her again. He didn't know when she was leaving to go back to Ohio. Jim started to panic, and then realized that, certainly, his cousin Andrea would have her phone number. He still felt a loss and kicked himself for not pursuing that information while they were together.

Jim called the taxidermy shop to make sure the taxidermist was there, and then took his and Andrea's deer heads over to the shop. It was getting toward suppertime when he finally got home. It was Wednesday evening, and officially he was still "off duty" until Thursday, but it was prayer meeting night, and a prayer meeting is where he wanted to be. He wondered if George and Andrea would go as well. They normally went on Wednesday nights but, under the circumstances, they might stay at home. If they did go, would Susan come too? She certainly wouldn't stay by herself.

Without hesitation, Jim picked up the phone and called George and Andrea's. When Andrea answered the phone, Jim asked, "Are you all going to prayer meeting tonight?"

Andrea laughed. "What do you think? Of course we will be there.

Inwardly, Jim sighed with relief and excitement. Audibly, he simply said, "All right. See you there. Thanks." As he hung up the phone, a smile came over his face. He could get the information himself.

After Jim had left, George and Andrea started putting things away and carrying the dirty clothes to the utility room. Andrea looked at Susan. "We have a spare bedroom for you," she said and showed her where it was. "The bath is across the hall, and there won't be anybody else in the house to run into during the night."

"Thanks," Susan replied. All of a sudden, she turned and looked at Andrea, a look of surprise and enthusiasm on her face. Andrea stopped and raised her eyebrows.

"What . . . what day is today?" Susan asked.

"This is Wednesday."

"Tomorrow. Tomorrow is the day," Susan whispered.

"The day for . . . what?" Andrea asked, and then inwardly scolded herself for being so obtuse.

"It was two years ago tomorrow," Susan said. "I didn't know how I was going to get through these last few days leading up to tomorrow, or how I would live through tomorrow. That's why I came to see you. I needed your help so badly. I knew that you would be able to help me, and you really have helped me." Tears welled up in Susan's eyes. "But instead of the last three days being some of the hardest and most depressing days of my life, I feel as though they've been some of the happiest and most joyous days of my life."

Andrea took Susan into her arms. For a long moment they stood there, holding each other. "God wants us to move on, Susan," Andrea said. "Of course, that's easy for me to say. I haven't been through the pain and suffering that you have. But I know that one cannot live in the past. I can sympathize for you, but not empathize with you. I want you to know that you have so much going for you."

They stood there for moments more, until Susan pulled away and looked into Andrea's eyes. "You're the best friend I've ever had," she said. "Thanks for being such a good friend."

Andrea gave her another hug. "You've certainly been a friend as well, Susan, and I'm glad you came. I'm thankful you had the freedom to come, and I'm happy everything has worked out the way it has. Let's get a light supper before we go to church this evening."

"Is it the church where Jim is the minister?" Susan asked.

"Yes, it is," Andrea replied.

"And will Jim be there?"

"Oh, yes, he'll be there. He's already called to see whether or not we're going."

Susan smiled. "I get to see him again . . . and then, I suppose, I need to be going home."

Andrea looked at Susan. "Our home is your home. You can stay as long as you wish."

Susan gave a contented sigh. "Andrea, you're so wonderful, and George is so kind. Let me help you fix supper. It feels good to be alive again."

Chapter 11

Jim arrived at the church half an hour before the service started. Pastor Burns was already there in his office, so Jim poked his head through the door. The senior pastor looked up and smiled. "Hi, Jim. Did you have a good vacation?"

"I think it's the best I've ever had. Three wonderful days."

"Good," Pastor Burns nodded. "Now that you've been on the mountain top, you can help us walk through the valley."

Jim looked at Pastor Burns. "How has the tenor of the congregation been during the last several days?"

"The congregation has a lot of growing to do. For some, it's easy to forgive and go on. For others, it's not so easy. There are those who are demanding that we take steps to ensure the safety them and their family, or they'll leave. As I told you on the phone, we need to call the pastors' council and the deacons together and come up with a plan that's biblical and satisfactory to the people in our congregation."

"It sounds like a lot of work," Jim replied. "I do want to chat with you for a couple of minutes after the service, if I could."

"I'll be around," Pastor Burns said with raised eyebrows.

Jim nodded and eased out of the door. The pastor watched him go. In the short amount of time that Jim had been there, he had never before seen the sparkle that was in Jim's eyes. "I thought he went hunting," he commented to himself, and then chuckled, "I wonder what kind of deer he found."

Jim was pleased when a few minutes later George, Andrea and Susan came into the church. The prayer meeting was held in a big circle, and Jim sat next to Susan, who was sitting beside Andrea and George. Jim leaned over and looked at Andrea and George. "One of you clowns owes me 200 bucks," he stated.

A questioning look came over their faces. "What do you mean?" George asked.

"You didn't give me the money for the deposit on Andrea's deer head."

Susan leaned back so that Jim and Andrea and George could talk among themselves. She enjoyed feeling the nearness of Jim's face to hers.

"Whoops!" George said. "Sorry about that." He reached into his pocket and pulled out two 100-dollar bills. "There, I have my half paid. Andrea, the rest is yours."

"When will you need it?" Andrea asked Jim.

"Oh, six, seven, eight months from now."

"That will be fine," Andrea replied.

Jim took the two "Uncle Ben's" and, reaching into his back hip pocket, pulled out his wallet to put the bills in for safekeeping. "You've got to watch those folks," he said to Susan. "They'll get you every chance they can." Andrea laughed.

Pastor Burns was now standing in front of the circle to begin the evening meeting. As he watched Jim and Andrea, he noticed a young woman he hadn't seen before sitting between them. *I was right,* he thought. *I wonder what kind of deer hunting Jim has been up to.*

The hour flew by, and soon the service was over. Andrea looked over at Susan. "Sure wish I had some ice cream to eat," she said.

"Me, too," quipped Susan. "A little ice cream would go a long way."

George glanced at Jim and shrugged. Jim was smiling on the inside. Throughout the meeting he had been wondering how he could get a chance to talk with Susan, and yet, he was feeling awkward because he was out of the hunting-camp setting. "There are a few people I need to talk to first," Jim said to George, "but I can get away in about ten minutes. I'll meet you all at the ice cream stand."

"Sounds good," Andrea said. Just then, Jim's parents walked up.

"How did the hunting go, Jim?" they asked.

"Great," said Jim. "I shot a nice ten-pointer." He looked from his parents over to Susan. "Dad, Mom, this is Susan Handley. She ended up in Pennsylvania with us the past few days. She is one of Andrea's good friends, and she got a good dose of what a hunting camp is."

Jim's parents shook Susan's hand. The "glad to meet you" phrases were exchanged, and then Jim left the little group and headed for the pastor's office. Once there, he closed the door. He wasn't sure what he wanted to say to Pastor Burns or how to say it, but being in the position that he was in—one in which his life was on display for the whole congregation—he felt that he needed some advice on what to do next with his relationship with Susan. He felt bashful, not knowing how to approach the subject with his senior pastor.

When Jim started to speak he was rewarded with a big smile from Pastor Burns. "You say you went hunting these past several days, right, Jim?"

"Yep, sure did," Jim replied.

"Did you do any good?"

"Sure did. I got a wall-hanger ten-pointer and a doe."

"And what else?"

"Well, that's all," said Jim, a bit puzzled. "That's all I had a license for."

"Hmm. Are you sure that's the only doe you found?" Pastor Burns asked with a twinkle in his eyes.

Jim quickly realized that he was reading him like a book. "How do I handle this?" he asked. "I don't know the young lady very well. Everyone will be looking and watching. I feel like my life will be on parade."

Pastor Burns laughed softly. "You are correct, Jim. Your life will be on parade. What you have to do is continue to live a godly life and pursue your dreams. If you have any questions, I'm always here for you."

Jim smiled. "Thanks for your support," he said, and then turned and left. When he walked back into the sanctuary, he saw that most of the people had left. Andrea and George and Susan had already gone as well, so he got in his Cherokee and headed for the ice cream stand. When Jim drove up, he found them in line getting ready to order. Jim pinched himself. *Am I really alive? Is this really happening?* he thought. Inwardly, he prayed, "God, I think I must be falling in love, and I don't even really know this person. She sure seems like an awfully nice person. Please give me wisdom and guide my footsteps. Help me to go slow. Help me to be sensitive to Your will."

Jim piled out of his Cherokee and walked over to where the others were getting ready to order. "I'll take a banana split," he said.

"Sounds good," Susan said.

George and Andrea nodded. "We'll make it four of them."

When they sat down to eat their banana splits, an awkward silence fell over the group. As Jim slowly ate, the different flavors of the ice cream tasted good, and he wondered what the next half-hour would bring. Finally, cranking up his courage, he looked at Susan and asked, "When do you have to go home?"

"I'm not sure," she said. "Most likely a couple of days from now."

"And, exactly, where is home, besides Ohio?"

"Outside of Columbus, about nine hours away."

"Nine hours," Jim said quietly. "Do you have a phone number? I need to let you know how Andrea is acting so that you can keep up with all of her mischief and treachery." Jim knew it sounded like a lame statement, but he didn't know what else to say. He looked at Andrea and George.

George was staring at him as if to say, "Come on, you blockhead, quit being so stupid. Tell her you want her phone number because you want it!"

"Andrea has my phone number, and I'd be glad to give it to you as well. I certainly would enjoy talking with you from time to time. I do need to know how George and Andrea are behaving."

Andrea slurped her banana split loudly. "I behave just fine," she said with a full mouth of ice cream. Everyone laughed.

"So, when do you preach?" Susan asked Jim.

"I normally preach the first Sunday of each month, and it looks as if that will be next Sunday or the following. I'll have to get a calendar to make sure."

"Well, I'd like to hear you preach. If you preach this Sunday, I may hang around, if George and Andrea don't kick me out." She looked over at the couple, knowing full well that she could stay as long as she wished.

Jim wanted to ask for her address, too, but, somehow, he felt that enough had been said. He would get enough ribbing from Andrea and George as it was. He had her phone number. He could call her and get her mailing and email address later.

They took their time eating their banana splits. Neither Jim nor Susan wanted the evening to end, but finally George said, "I've got to get up early to go to the grocery store tomorrow, and I'm tired. It's time for us to go."

"Yes, and I need to go to work," Andrea said. "There are sick people who need my special loving care."

"I guess you're right," Susan said. "It's different for me. I haven't worked these past two years."

Jim looked at Susan. He wondered how she could afford not to work. Was she on disability? And why wasn't she working . . . so many issues crowded his mind. He liked what he saw, but he had so many questions.

Susan answered some of them without prompting. "Ever since my husband died, I've had a hard time adjusting," she said. "At times I have been on medication for my nerves, for stress. With the different insurance policies that my husband had, I've been able to survive without having to work."

Jim's heart went out to Susan. How he wished he could hug her again, but he knew it was not the right time.

They pushed back their chairs. George and Andrea said goodnight and walked toward their vehicle. Susan hung back, and Jim grabbed her hands.

"I'll be in touch, Susan," he said.

"I'd like that Jim," she said. "You've been so kind these last several days, and I have really appreciated your friendship."

Jim gave her hands a squeeze and then, together, they walked out to George's car. "Gotta go to work myself tomorrow," Jim said, breaking the silence. "I've got people to visit, sermons to write, problems to solve; it's a rough life, but somebody has to do it."

George laughed. "Yeah, well, when you really want to work, come on down to the grocery store and I'll find you something to do."

"I've bagged more than one head of lettuce," Jim said. "I could do it again."

They said their goodbyes, and Jim watched as George drove out of sight. He drove home slowly, wondering how his feelings could be so obvious that his pastor could pick up on what was bothering him. Yes, he thought he'd gotten more than one kind of "deer" in Pennsylvania.

He looked in the rear view mirror and then followed the lights in front of him as he drove home. He was a mixed bag of emotions. On the one hand, he was excited about the prospects of a relationship with someone who seemed like a very nice person; but on the other, he was concerned about his congregation, which was hurting and torn.

Once he got home, Jim flipped on the television to watch a ballgame before going to bed. He watched the game, but his mind kept wondering and turning. What did the future hold? Next year at this time, would he be able to share the bedroom in the hunting cabin instead of having to sleep on the couch? And if that were the case, would he be sharing it with the person who was in that bedroom this year?

A smile came across his face. He certainly hoped so.

Chapter 12

The next morning found the group going their separate ways. George was up early and back at his grocery store. Andrea needed to work the 7:00 A.M. to 3 P.M. nursing shift. Before she left the house, she wrote a note to Susan telling her to feel free to find whatever breakfast she wanted and to spend the day as she liked. Andrea said that she would be home soon after 3:30.

Jim was also up early. He needed to go to the hospital and visit with several patients from the church. With a 200-member congregation, there was always someone in the hospital. The evening before, he had received a prayer request about someone who was in the hospital, so he knew whom he needed to visit. Normally, on Mondays, Jim and Pastor Burns did hospital visitation together. Other than that, they took turns visiting on alternate days—Thursday was Jim's normal day for hospital visitation. The senior pastor, if not otherwise busy with congregational duties, spent his mornings at the church in his study, where he would pray, study the Bible, work on his sermons, counsel people and so forth. A man had to wear many hats to be the leader of a flock.

Susan got up around 7:30 and ate a bowl of cereal, wondering what she would do for the day. She thought about Jim and where he was and what he was doing. Somehow, she was drawn back to the church. With nothing better to do, she found her way back to where they were the evening before. She stopped in the parking lot, but she didn't see Jim's Cherokee. A sense of disappointment, but also relief, spread over her. She wanted to see into his world—to see what made him tick—and without him there, she would be freer to sense the flavor of the church, empty though it was.

She walked up to the front door and was surprised to find it open. Just off the vestibule were several doors. One was marked "office" on a plaque above the door. It was open, and she heard someone inside. Immediately feeling less sure of herself, she forced herself to walk toward the door. She hesitated at the threshold.

Nearby, the church secretary looked up and, seeing her, flashed a smile. "Hi," she said. "May I help you?"

"Um, well, I just wanted to look around," Susan said.

The secretary smiled. "Let me get our pastor for you."

Susan acknowledged with a shake of her head that that would be fine. Then she began to wonder if Jim actually was there. The secretary had said "pastor," not "assistant pastor." That could mean either one of them. Susan couldn't believe that she was being so bold.

The secretary led Susan around the corner to another office that had "senior pastor" on the door nameplate. The secretary knocked lightly, and a voice from within said, "Come in."

The secretary opened the door. "Hi, pastor. There's someone here who wants to see around the church." Looking at Susan, she added, "I'm sorry, ma'am, I didn't ask you your name."

"It's Susan," she replied. "I just wanted to see your church and check out the layout and see what it was like."

Pastor Burns smiled. "Come in."

The secretary went back to her office, and Susan went in and sat on the edge of a chair. Pastor Burns returned to his chair behind the desk. "Now," he said to Susan, "what brings you here? How may I help you?"

His kind smile helped Susan to relax. "I just felt drawn to come," she said. "I'm visiting George and Andrea, and a few days ago I ended up going hunting with them."

"With Jim?" asked Pastor Burns.

Susan felt her ears start to burn. "Yes, he was there. He certainly is a fine gentleman."

Pastor Burns looked at Susan for a moment with a twinkle in his eye. "So, you went hunting with Jim, George and Andrea these last several days. Now, how do you know George and Andrea?"

"Andrea and I went through nursing school together," Susan answered. "She has always been a dear friend and, well, I have been through a couple of rough years. I needed someone to help me and to support me in a time of need, and I thought of Andrea. I live in Ohio. I foolishly came unannounced, right when they were planning on going hunting. Instead of disrupting their plans, they invited me to go along."

Pastor Burns sat there with his hands folded, tapping his fingertips together as he listened. Susan drew quiet, not sure what else to say. The pastor looked at her for a few more seconds and then said, "So, you're the extra 'doe' that ended up in camp."

Susan blushed. "Yes, I guess I am."

"Jim told me he got a couple of nice deer, but I knew there was something else eating at him. Tell me more about yourself, Susan. I have time to listen."

Pastor Burns' manner helped Susan relax, and she was able to tell him about the past two years of her life and the struggles she had been through. Suddenly, realizing that it was Thursday, a wrenching pain crossed her face. "Today is the two-year anniversary of my husband's death," she explained. "I didn't know how I would be able to get through these days. Andrea and her husband, George, and

Jim and the other couple in the cabin have truly made these last several days happy ones for me. I've finally come to grips with my hurt and my bitterness and have turned them over to Jesus. The weight is off my shoulders. Jim has been very kind to me these last few days. It feels as if I can live again. But I can't stay here and impose on Andrea and George, even though they have been so kind and Andrea told me to stay as long as I like. I guess I was drawn here today because I would like to know more about Jim. In one way, I was disappointed when his Cherokee wasn't sitting outside. In another way, I was relieved. I have so many mixed emotions."

The senior pastor continued to sit there, his eyes half-closed and his fingers tapping each other. He had a smile on his face.

"Christ has given me a peace," Susan continued. "I believe that I can go on now and have hope. Instead of being in despair on this second anniversary of my husband's death, I have a sense of strength and motivation that I haven't experienced in a long, long time. In addition to that, there's something about Jim that draws me to him. He's a minister, and I would have never dreamed of being associated with someone like that. I don't really know if anything will come of this. Of course, I will let Jim take the initiative if a relationship is to develop. But, if it does, how should I react? What should I do? It seems it would take a very special person to be a helpmate for a pastor."

A big grin came across Pastor Burns' face. "Jim is a fine young man. His heart is, unquestionably, in the right place. He's kind and considerate—everyone likes him. He does have two big faults about him, though."

"Oh?" responded Susan with eyebrows raised.

"Yes," the pastor said. "Fault number one: he's single. Fault number two: he loves to hunt."

Susan laughed. "Well, I don't know if I can help him with either of those," she said self-consciously.

"Jim is A-1 and a mighty fine young man." Pastor Burns' mind began to whirl as he mused to himself about the events of the past fifteen hours. "A week ago, I would never have dreamed that Jim would come to me with questions about to how to build a relationship, considering his current capacity here at the church. And, undoubtedly, I would never have dreamed that the young lady, whom I had never met before, would come and ask me questions about Jim."

The pastor paused to collect his thoughts but continued quickly so as not to make Susan uncomfortable with a lengthy silence. "Your testimony of what you've been through is touching and sad. But it's inspiring and uplifting, too. For you to be able to come to grips with the tough things that life has dealt you, accept Christ's will and plan for your life, give it all to Christ, and then let Him give you freedom from your burdens is exhilarating and moving. Certainly, a couple of years are long enough to begin to dream and to begin to hope. Susan, if Jim does pursue a relationship with you, just let yourself be pursued in a godly way. We'll see what God's plans are for you and Jim. You live in Ohio. I know that seems like an obstacle, but I know that things will work out if they are in God's will. I don't know what all will happen, but it will definitely be enjoyable to watch from the sidelines. I can only wish you God's grace and His blessing on your life. I believe that our church has some tough times and some exciting times ahead, and it will be interesting to see how things progress."

"This has all happened so quickly," Susan declared. "I don't really know what to think. Maybe I'm reading more into the situation than what is really there, but I wanted to come and just see what the church is like and to know Jim in this capacity."

Pastor Burns stood up. "Let me show you the church," he said. "Jim will return later this morning, but I don't think he'll catch you here if we take just fifteen to twenty minutes to go through the facilities."

"Thank you," replied Susan. "I don't want him to think that I'm chasing him."

An hour later, Susan was back at Andrea's house. She fixed herself a salad for lunch and sat down in the living room. Finding a book to read, she picked it up and began to browse. She felt at peace. She was content.

Chapter 13

Sunday morning was Jim's turn to preach. He had struggled over how he wanted to present his sermon. It wasn't often that he preached two times in row, but with Pastor Burns being on vacation the week before, Jim had the chance to follow up on his sermon from the past Sunday. When Jim walked into the sanctuary, it seemed that the congregation was extra full that morning. Jim had a song in his heart. He had worked hard to prepare his sermon and felt that it was something that God wanted him to share. He wanted to continue his theme from a week ago on forgiveness, growth and caring for one another.

As Jim had struggled in getting his sermon ready that week, he kept thinking back to Susan, daydreaming about her gentle ways and the kiss on his hand. He hadn't talked to her since Wednesday evening, and it seemed that the last three days had been awfully long. He wasn't sure if she was still visiting or if she had gone back to Ohio. When the time came for him to preach, he stood and looked out over the congregation. His eyes searched for George and Andrea, and a thrill ran through him when he saw that Susan was sitting with them. The smile he saw on her face bolstered him. "Lord, help me," he breathed. "Help me to keep my mind fixed on You. Remove my self-thoughts and help me to present the message that You want presented this morning."

Jim delivered his sermon, and then sat down as the announcements were made at the close of the service. He listened as the announcer stated that in three weeks, a congregational meeting would be held for those who were interested in discussing how the church should care for one particular church attendee. *An attendee who some people think is less desirable than any other sinner saved by grace,* Jim thought. As he listened to the announcer conclude, he contemplated how he wanted to help people see and understand that sin is sin.

How could anyone who has experienced the saving grace of Jesus Christ be so unwilling to forgive someone else of his or her sins? Jim thought. *Even a convicted criminal who has accepted Christ is just as much a child of God as anyone else who has received the free gift of salvation. Will he be tempted to sin? Of course, the same as someone who is thirty pounds overweight might be tempted to eat a second piece of chocolate pie.* Jim thought through a whole array of sins that people so easily commit yet wave off and excuse. Somehow, some sins seemed to be more terrible than others. Of course, it was true that while a sin to one's self was bad enough, a sin against another definitely needed to be guarded against.

Jim looked forward to the meeting in three weeks and wondered what the outcome would be. What solutions could calm the people's fears and help them understand the safety and protection of the church? He also wondered about the gentleman getting out of prison and the protection that he would need.

Jim went to the back of the sanctuary when the service was over and shook peoples' hands as they left. His eyes lit up when George, Andrea and Susan filed past him. He took Susan's hand and shook it, and then, on impulse, brought her hand to his mouth and placed a light kiss on the back of it. Susan blushed. "I see you stayed until today, Susan," he said. "I'm glad you're here."

"You had a fine sermon, Jim," she murmured.

Andrea teasingly pushed Susan out of the way and grabbed Jim's hand. "Good job, cousin," she said. She turned to George. "Now, where are we going to eat?"

George laughed. "Well, the grocery store isn't open today, and my deli is the only place for good food around here."

"Don't be so egotistical, George," Andrea scolded playfully. "I'm sure we can find some place decent to eat."

Pastor Burns stood across from the vestibule, also shaking hands and chatting with people. He watched the exchange between the four friends. It looked as if the little love arrows were flying, and he breathed a prayer to God as he shook hands with those around him. None of them realized how much he knew about the drama that was beginning to play out in front of him. He thanked God for His wisdom and for His guidance and prayed that He would continue to lead.

"So, where are we going to eat?" Andrea asked again.

"I put a roast in the oven with potatoes and carrots before I left for church this morning," Jim said. "I would be glad to have you all come and eat at my house, unless you'd prefer to eat out somewhere."

"Deer roast?" Susan quipped. "I guess after watching you all shoot them, the least I could help you do is eat the meat—and I would get to see where you live."

"Okay," Jim said, "But realize I didn't clean up for company this morning."

George laughed. "Right, we're company. We won't even be able to get into the place, as much of a dump as it is."

Andrea punched George in the waist. "You know that's not true. Jim keeps an immaculate house—for a bachelor."

Jim felt his ears begin to burn, and Susan laughed. "I want to know what a good country meal tastes like at a bachelor's house," she said.

"Then follow me," Jim said with a wave of his hand.

"Oh, we'll follow you," George said, "even though I think we know the way there."

Jim looked at Susan. "I guess if you ride with me, you can ride shotgun. George and Andrea would make you sit in the back seat of their vehicle."

Susan looked over at Andrea, "Oh, go on, Susan. Don't be bashful," Andrea said with a twinkle in her eyes. "Anyway, Jim is right—I'm certainly not going to let you sit up front next to George. That's my spot."

Susan turned to Jim. "If you don't mind, I'll be glad to ride with you. And I'm hungry. Let's go!"

They walked to their vehicles, and Jim opened the door of his Cherokee for Susan, helping her in by holding her hand. He carefully closed the door and walked around behind the vehicle. Pastor Burns watched from the vestibule doors of the church. "How big a roast do you have in the oven, Jim?"

Jim looked up and smiled. "Enough for six," he said. "You all come on!"

"Don't mind if we do, assistant Rev," Pastor Burns remarked cleverly. "Don't mind if we do."

"Why, Reverend William Burns," his wife scolded. "Shame on you, inviting yourself out for lunch."

"Mrs. Mary Burns," the pastor replied. "This is the best invite I've ever wrangled. We're going to have fun."

Mrs. Burns looked at her husband and all of a sudden realized what Jim had said about there being enough for six. Just as suddenly, she realized that she had seen Jim help someone into his Cherokee. Her husband read the question in her eyes.

Pastor Burns smiled at his wife with a mischievous grin. "We're going to go eat lunch and maybe do a few other things, too. Let's go."

Susan was all eyes as they drove up to Jim's home. She was curious about where Jim lived, and she realized that what she would see would give her a lot of information about the character of this man who was beginning to interest her so. George and Andrea pulled in behind Jim and looked back to see the third vehicle approaching the house.

After they had gotten out of their cars, George looked at Jim and said, "Now you're in for it. We'll get you taken care of quick."

Jim reached down, picked up a stone out of the lane and tossed it at George. "Behave yourself, George. Pastor Burns invited himself to lunch. I couldn't say no."

They walked into Jim's house, and the smell of the roast made their saliva glands work overtime. "Come on," Andrea said to Susan, "let's help this poor bachelor get this meal ready."

Jim tried to stand in Andrea's way, but she pushed him aside. "You know that I know what I'm doing. Get out of the way and let us women take care of things."

Jim went back to the door and let in Pastor Burns and his wife. "Come on in," he said. "We have plenty to eat."

"Smells good," Pastor Burns said. Mrs. Burns went straight to the kitchen to see what she could do to help. The men stayed in the living room.

Andrea took the meat out, and Mrs. Burns offered to carve it. Susan looked up. "What else needs to be done?" she asked.

"You can get out the plates and the silverware and set the table," Andrea said, "and then get the potatoes and carrots out of the pan and I'll help you make some gravy with the remaining broth. This won't take long; we'll soon be ready to eat."

The men stood in the living room, and an awkward silence fell over them. "Well, sit down and make yourselves at home," said Jim. "The football game is on in ten minutes. I hope the 'Deadskins' can beat the Giants today."

"'Deadskins'," George laughed. "You're right."

"They'll make the playoffs this year, you watch," said Pastor Burns. "They're already eight and six. Two more wins in these last couple of weeks will put them in the playoffs."

"I hope so," George said.

The men continued to talk football until Mrs. Burns stuck her head into the living room. "All right, guys, it's time to eat."

"It sure does smell good," Jim said. "I don't know why I can't have maids like this all the time to work in my kitchen."

"All you have to do is ask," George said.

Jim punched him in the ribs. Susan looked at George and then back at Jim. *What would it be like to be the queen of this kitchen?* she thought. More and more in the last couple of days, such thoughts were beginning to be appealing to her. She wondered if it would ever happen.

They sat down around the table, held hands and prayed and enjoyed the wonderful meal of roast venison, potatoes, carrots and gravy bread. "I didn't fix any dessert," Jim said. "I wasn't expecting company."

"Who's company?" Andrea teased. "And for dessert, I'll just have another piece of gravy bread."

"That sounds like a good idea," Susan said. "I would love to eat more meat as well, but I'm so full. I think I've gained five pounds this week."

George looked up. "Be careful how much weight you gain. You want to keep that pretty figure."

"That's right," Andrea said, "you don't want to look like a butterball."

Susan again felt her neck reddening and the heat rising on her ears. Jim looked at George and Andrea. "Leave the poor woman alone, you all. She looks fine to me."

"That's just it," George said. "The way she is looks just fine to you. You'd like to keep her that way."

Jim groaned. He decided to quickly change the subject. "The golden rule of this kitchen is that if you fix the meal, you also get to do the dishes."

The women laughed. "You men get out of here and watch your football game. We'll clean up."

The women spent the next twenty minutes cleaning off the table and washing and drying the dishes. Mrs. Burns asked Susan questions about where she had come from and how she had met Andrea. Andrea told how they had gone through nursing school together and how Susan had arrived on the spur of the moment at her and George's house. Mrs. Burns hurt inside when she heard of Susan's stress, frustration and agony over losing her husband, but she rejoiced when she heard of the fun and the healing that Susan had experienced at the hunting camp and by spending several days in George and Andrea's home. She smiled at the realization of what could be and thought of how nice a girl Susan seemed to be.

As the men continued to watch their football game, the women walked outside. "This place could use some more flower beds," Andrea said innocently.

"Don't rush things, Andrea," said Susan. "I'm going home tomorrow morning, remember?"

"Oh, you'll be back," Andrea said. "Christmastime is coming; it's only a month away."

Susan stopped with a faraway look in her eyes. Quietly, she mused, "I wonder what the next several months will bring."

"Pray a lot and listen to the Lord's still, small voice," Mrs. Burns said. "It's amazing how He works things out."

The men watched the game until halftime, and then Pastor Burns got up and stretched. "Well, gentlemen," he said, "I must take my wife home. We have some other plans for this evening, and I need to go home and rest and prepare for it."

The men walked out with the pastor and his wife. Jim and George stood there while the older couple drove away. "He's a fine minister," Jim said to no one in particular. Just then, the men heard the front door opening. Andrea and Susan came out and stood with them.

"Sure is a nice day," Andrea said. "We ought to be able to find something to do. We could always play cards."

"We could watch the rest of the football game," George offered, winking over his shoulder to his hopeful buddy.

"Oh, football!" Andrea complained. "There's more to life than football!"

Jim's cell phone rang, and he answered it. As he listened, a frown came over his face. He walked away from the others to have some privacy for the conversation. When he turned back toward them, they could see the concern on his face. Finally, he hung up and walked back to the three. "I guess my duties call. There's a couple from our church who are upset about a situation that's affecting our church body. They're insisting that I come over and talk. I tried to tell them that we'll have a formal meeting in several weeks, but they won't take no for an answer. So I told them I could come, but only for an hour, since there are other things I want to do yet today."

"Oh great," Andrea said. "I love being friends with a minister. Life is always so unpredictable. You can't plan anything."

"Now, Andrea," George said.

"Well, what do we do? I guess we might as well go home," Andrea said. She exchanged glances with Susan.

"If Jim's only going to be gone for a little over an hour," Susan said, "why don't you go on home? I'll stay here and let Jim bring me over to your house later on this evening." Andrea opened her mouth to protest, but Susan raised her hand and said, "No, I think that is what I would like to do. I can be here in the peace and quiet."

Jim looked at Susan. "I think that's a fine idea," he said. "I wanted to talk with you this evening anyway. I would like coming home and finding you here."

George winked at him. "Sure you would." He turned to Andrea. "Come on, dear, let's leave these youngsters alone. They have a busy afternoon ahead of them."

Jim apologized again for needing to run off, and then got into his Cherokee and drove away. After he had gone, Andrea asked Susan, "Are you sure you want to stay here by yourself?"

"Yes, I really do," Susan responded. "I would like very much to be here."

George nudged Andrea. "Come on, let's go. We'll get home in time to see the end of the football game."

Susan watched as George and Andrea got into their car and drove down the lane to the road. She looked around at the house and the flowers, taking in Jim's castle and feeling him in the air around her. She walked around the house, noticing how neatly the lawn was mowed. She noticed the size of his yard and the clothesline poles and clothesline. "I wonder who this man, Jim, really is?" she said to herself. "He surely is a unique individual."

Susan walked the rest of the way around the house and then went inside. In the kitchen, she saw how neat and in place everything was. She started down the hallway and stopped, wondering how far she should snoop in someone else's house, especially when that person wasn't there. However, the door to her right was open, and when she looked in she realized that it was Jim's study. As soon as she walked in, a sense of peace and calm came over her. She marveled at all the books on the shelves behind Jim's desk and noticed a couple of recliners in the room as well. She realized that it was a study room, a counseling room and a room where spiritual matters were conducted.

She sat in Jim's chair and looked at his desk. Then, standing up, she walked over to a row of books. Finding one that held her interest, she took it off the shelf and started paging through it. She flipped through a few pages and then, turning, walked over to one of the recliners. She pulled on the lever after sitting down, brought the leg rest up, tilted the chair back and began looking through the book, leafing from page to page. She felt as though she was in Jim's presence.

As she sat there, her mind began to wander. She had gotten past the two-year anniversary of her husband's death, and this last week, for the first time, she had felt like living again. What was the main cause of her healing? After a two-year struggle, fighting fear, anger and frustration, she realized that the major factor in her healing was being able to surrender herself to God, knowing that He knew what was best for her life. But how much had Jim played a part in helping her get to that point? Would God bring them together?

"I sure hope so," Susan said out loud to herself.

Susan startled. *What did you say to yourself?*

"I said, 'I sure hope so.'"

Susan couldn't believe the way she was thinking. Was it right? Was it wrong? Yet the still, small voice inside of her comforted her. "It has been two years, Susan. You're choosing to look forward, not backward. You're choosing to live, to laugh."

Susan smiled. Yes, what would it be like to be the queen of this house? What would it be like if she was here waiting, on a regular basis, for Jim to come home? She felt her pulse quicken as she thought about what it would be like—what it would be like to be in his arms, to be kissed by him, to be loved by him. Now she didn't fight the daydreaming but let her mind drift. The book in her arms fell forward against her chest, and her chin nodded forward, resting on top of the book. She was experiencing a peace and happiness that she hadn't felt in a couple of years. She sat there in the warmth, in the arms of God's love, totally relaxed.

Chapter 14

Jim spent forty minutes with the elderly couple from the church, talking with them and helping them understand that God is a God of love and forgiveness and that we are all sinners saved by His grace. He told them that all people have things in their past that they wouldn't want other people to know—things that would make others think less highly of them. He helped the couple understand that no matter what, as God's children, we are to love each other and give each other support so that we can grow and not fall into temptation. "After all," Jim said, "If we didn't support one another, what good would our church be? In fact, would we be a church at all if we said who could and who couldn't worship with us? If we selected our members, it would be like a country club."

Jim left the elderly couple at peace. He felt that he had helped them understand the Christian love that we are to show our fellow man. As he drove home, he thought of Susan; about the way he could see forever through her multi-colored eyes and the mystery they held. He thought of her light kiss upon his hand. *I hope she stayed at my place and waited for me to come back*, he thought. *How nice to have someone to go home to. God, is this the woman You have chosen for me?* He tried to rationalize the situation and look at the pros and cons of what he knew about Susan. Could one fall in love in only a week's time? Jim could hardly think so, but, subconsciously, he went down the list of things that made Susan attractive to him.

She certainly was beautiful on the outside, but that wasn't a reason to marry someone. He thought about the days he had spent with her at the deer camp, of her embarrassment over colliding with him in the dark. He realized that there were mischievous and fun-loving qualities about her by the way she responded to the general fun and teasing that they'd had in the camp. He realized that he enjoyed being with her. *But again,* he argued with himself, *just enjoying being with someone isn't a reason to fall in love. You have to step back and evaluate her character.* How aggressive was Susan? She'd been married before. Would she carry baggage around with her from that experience? Did that make her aggressive? Jim thought, again, about her picking up his hand and kissing it lightly. He wondered if being aggressive was a bad thing, even though, in her own way, she was sweet about it.

He tried to think of other negative aspects of her personality. How did she handle herself back at the house when he was called away unexpectedly? There would be many times in his ministry when he would be called away. In effect, he was on call 24/7. How would she respond to that in the years to come? Suddenly, Jim laughed at himself and said out loud, "What are you thinking, man? Do you think Susan could be the one?" He looked into the rear view mirror and pulled it around so he could see himself. "Well, could she be the one or not?" he asked himself again. "I don't know," was the response he gave to the face in the mirror. "But if she is, I certainly want to be the type of man to merit her love."

Jim pulled into his driveway and looked at his house. It was the same house, same yard, same front door. No one opened the door to come out. A twinge of disappointment crept across him. Did Susan not stay? He had secretly hoped that she would open the door and be standing there, waiting for him to get home.

He opened his front door and walked inside. The house was still and quiet. He went to the kitchen. It was empty. He went to the living room. The TV was still on. There were a couple more minutes to go in the game, and it looked as though the Redskins would win. *Apparently, Susan didn't stay,* he thought.

He went to his bedroom. *She certainly wouldn't have gone there,* he said to himself. He started to call out her name, but then realized how foolish that would be. So he walked back out to the kitchen, and as he passed his study he saw her sitting in the recliner with her chin resting on the top edge of the book. He stopped to look at her. A warm spot began to widen within his heart, and a smile broke across his face. She had stayed.

He tiptoed up to her and stood beside her, wondering if just his presence would cause her to sense that she was no longer alone. He stood there watching for thirty seconds, but still she dozed. On an impulse, he leaned down and lightly kissed her forehead. Instantly, her head raised up, her eyes popped open and, with a startled expression on her face, she looked up at Jim. Her foggy brain tried to comprehend where she was and what the situation was. She realized that she'd been kissed on her forehead and looked up into sparkling eyes that couldn't conceal the reason for the grin on his face. She smiled. "You're home," she said.

"Yes," Jim said, "I'm home, and I'm glad to see that you're here, too."

Immediately, Susan felt embarrassed. She got up out of the recliner, closed the book and put it back on the shelf. She smiled. "I guess I was relaxed enough that I went to sleep."

"I'm glad you were," Jim said. "Let's get something to drink. Do you like your tea sweet or unsweetened?"

"Unsweetened, and not too strong."

"Do you want some mint in it?"

"That sounds good to me."

Jim went to the kitchen. On the "plus side" of his list, he mentally added, *Likes unsweetened mint tea that's weak. It's a small thing, but still important. She must be some girl.*

Jim and Susan sat in the kitchen on barstools around the counter, drinking their iced tea. Jim looked into Susan's eyes and drank in the depth of what he found there. "When are you going home?" he asked.

"I need to leave in the morning," Susan replied. "I've been here for a week, and I don't want to wear out my welcome at Andrea and George's."

"I was afraid you would say that," Jim said. "Somehow, it won't be the same when you leave. Of course, you won't wear out Andrea and George's welcome, but I certainly understand you not wanting to stay there for a prolonged period of time. I sure do hate to see you go. It . . . it won't be the same when you're not here."

Susan swirled the remaining ice cubes in her glass. "This has been the best week I've had in the last two years, Jim, and you have, without a doubt, played a big part in it. All the stress, the anger, the hurt, the depression . . . somehow, this week, I've finally been able to turn them over to God and say that I'm ready to move on and begin a new chapter of my life."

Jim reached over and picked up one of Susan's fingers. Rubbing it, he looked in her eyes and said, "I'm glad that you came. I've never known what it was like to feel so content to be with a woman before."

Susan laughed and stood up. "Now, Jim, you're trying to kid me. Surely you've had friendships and lady friends in the past."

Jim felt the heat rising on his neck and his ears growing red and hot. "No, Susan, I've never found anyone who made me feel relaxed or comfortable when I'm around her. I've never found anyone who's made me want to be with her. You gave me your telephone number. I would love to have your email address and your mailing address. I don't want us to go our separate ways. I don't want this to be an ending. I want it to be the building-on of a beginning."

Susan looked at Jim and quietly said, "So do I, Jim. That would be nice."

Jim stood up and walked over to Susan. He put his arm around her waist and, laying his face up beside hers, gave her a gentle squeeze. Susan didn't try to pull away. She marveled in the rightness of the feeling of having someone cherish her. They stood that way for less than a minute, but Jim felt as though it was an hour—a blissful hour.

Jim drew away and, looking into Susan's eyes, asked, "What do you want to do this evening? It's still early. We don't have an evening service.

Susan looked at him, her eyes sparkling. "We could talk about when we could get together again."

Jim smiled. "I don't have much vacation time left this year, but I do have several days around the New Year. I could come to Ohio to see you."

"What would you normally be doing around that time of year?" Susan asked.

Jim gave her a sheepish grin. "Would deer hunting be a bad answer?"

"More deer hunting?"

"Well, I do enjoy it. I will confess that I've killed four this year: two here in Virginia and two in Pennsylvania. But across the Blue Ridge Mountains, rifle season continues through the first Saturday of January, and we like hunting there as well. That's when we harvest some doe meat for good eating."

Susan laughed. "If I could make the trip in November, I certainly should be able to make it at the end of December. This week has been such an eye-opener for me that I would love to spend a couple more days with you hunting. Do you have a cabin there as well? What's the layout?"

"We have friends who live on a farm, and they open up their home to us. We barge in and bring food and sleeping bags and spend a couple of days visiting with them. We hunt, play Rook, relax . . ."

"Would there be room for me?"

"We'll make room. If I have to sleep on the couch, we'll make room."

Susan smiled and wrinkled up her nose. "That might not be too comfortable."

"Well, I have slept in a chair before," Jim retorted, "and to have you along, I would do it again. I would sleep on the floor if I needed to."

Susan laughed again. "You really wouldn't mind if I came and enjoyed those days with you?"

"It wouldn't be the same if you weren't there," he chuckled.

Jim and Susan spent the evening talking about their lives, their dreams, their families and their backgrounds. Susan told Jim how she was an only daughter, and how her parents, now deceased, had lived in Ohio all of their lives. Jim shared how his parents were still living and were close by. They enjoyed the evening so much that it was a surprise to both of them when they realized that it was heading toward 11 o'clock. "Mercy!" Susan gasped. "I hope Andrea's not waiting up for me."

Jim grinned. "If she is, then it will give her some practice. She'll see what it'll be like to wait up for her children one day."

"And here I am being the bad daughter, being out too late."

"Well, at least you were in good company."

Susan looked at him and smiled. "It certainly hasn't been bad. In fact, I think I can say that it's been very, very good."

Jim felt an unexpected rush of emotions. He looked into Susan's eyes, trying to read all that he could in them. He didn't mind staring near as much now as he had a week ago. Susan noticed what he was doing and smiled back. "Your dark brown eyes are just brown, Jim, but they look awfully nice to me."

Jim grinned. "Mine are just brown, not multicolored like yours."

"But I can still see into them, and I like what I see," Susan said softly.

Jim got up and reached for his coat. "Well, I think it's time I got you back to Andrea and George's."

On the way to Andrea's house, Jim reached over and picked up Susan's hand. Susan gave a contented sigh. She wondered if Jim might try to kiss her when they parted for the night at Andrea's front door. She also wondered how she would respond. Having been married, she'd certainly been kissed many, many times, but she wondered if Jim had ever kissed a woman before. It was hard to comprehend that he had not, being twenty-seven years of age, but he had also told her that she was the first woman with whom he'd ever been really comfortable around. Susan wondered, again, if he would attempt such a thing. She craved to be held, to be loved. Part of the agony of the last two years was not having a protective arm around her, or tender kisses, or loving hugs. She missed a husband's love.

They said very little on the drive, both pondering their own thoughts. *What do I do now?* Jim wondered. Susan was a widow and therefore knew the ins and outs of love, but he wasn't sure what to do. He didn't like the idea of doing anything that might cause her to pull back from him.

"Call me when you get back to Ohio," Jim said quietly as they pulled up to Andrea's lane. "An eight-hour drive is a long drive for a lady to make by herself."

"Yes," Susan murmured, "it is, and I really wish I didn't need to go, but I do need to go home."

"But you will be back in about a month."

"Yes, I positively will do my best, if the snow doesn't lie too deep."

As Jim stood on George's porch, getting ready to open the door for Susan, he looked at her and said, "I really don't know what to do or how to behave, but I would sure love to give you a hug."

Susan looked up at him and smiled. "I would sure love to let you."

Jim took her in his arms and laid his cheekbone, still a little tender, against the top of her head. She rested her head easily against his shoulder. He reveled in the feelings that he had for Susan, drinking in the lovely fragrance of her sweet, yet subtle perfume. He lowered his head and placed a kiss on her cheek. Susan turned, and their faces were just inches apart. "I've never kissed a woman before," Jim murmured, "and somehow I always felt that if and when I did, it would mean much more than just showing passion or desire. You may think me odd or old-fashioned, but if I were to kiss you, to me that would mean something more than what I believe we're ready for at this time."

Susan backed up, and Jim straightened up as well. "I always felt that when a girl agreed to marry me, then I would kiss her," Jim said tenderly.

Susan looked at him with tears glistening in the corners of her eyes. "I think that's very admirable, Jim. So, in that case, no, I won't let you kiss me, but maybe, some day . . ."

"Maybe, some day," Jim echoed Susan. "The way I feel now, I certainly hope so."

In the light of the porch, Susan stood on her tiptoes and, with her hand, turned Jim's face away from her. She kissed him lightly on the cheek. "Until then," she said.

Jim responded by giving her another hug. "Until then," he murmured.

Suddenly, the porch light flashed off and on. From inside, they heard Andrea remark, "Okay, kids, break it up." Then they heard Andrea and George laugh.

"The lousy bums have been spying on us!" said Jim.

"Oh, me," said Susan, "I feel like a school girl being caught with my hand in the cookie jar."

"We'll never live this down," said Jim, "but then, maybe we don't want to."

Susan opened the door and walked into the house.

"Come on in, Jim," said George. "We need to hear what's going on."

"It's late," Jim said. "I think it's time for me to go home."

"I guess you're right," said Andrea, "but believe me, we're going to hear more about this!" She and George laughed again.

Jim simply put his hands in his pockets and walked back to the car. But inside, a feeling was glowing that he'd never experienced before. He put the key in the ignition, started the car, and then stopped. He turned the inside light on, pulled the rearview mirror down and looked at himself. "I think," he said to the mirror, "that I must be falling in love."

Chapter 15

The next couple of weeks sped by. Christmas was drawing near. Every evening, Jim went to his computer to check his emails, and he was always delighted to receive letters from Susan. He wrote back every day, telling her what was going on and sharing with her his feelings, his hurts, his joys and his dealings with the people of the congregation. The congregational meeting was now only a few days away, and Jim asked Susan to be in prayer for the spiritual welfare of the people as well as the gentleman getting out of prison who wanted to be a part of their fellowship.

Susan was thrilled as well to get Jim's emails each evening. She felt that she could feel Jim's presence through them, and she enjoyed listening to his voice when he called on the phone. In her responses, Susan told of her life in Ohio. Her days were filled with activities, and the doctor was saying that she no longer needed to take a lot of the medication that she had been on. She was excited and felt like living again, and she shared her feelings and thoughts with Jim. She also shared in depth how the horrors of depression and anxiety had drained away her strength and joy the past two years.

Susan wanted to give something to Jim for Christmas, and she felt no reserve about doing so. But how personal a gift should it be? Wondering what to do, she called Andrea and told her about the past few weeks and how elated she was with the way that she was healing and living life again. Andrea listened and waited until Susan finally ran out of breath. Then she simply asked, "So, Susan, do you love him?"

"Oh Andrea," Susan remarked, "Do I love him? I was in love with my husband, and we had a good life. But thinking back, I don't remember ever feeling the thrill, excitement and anticipation of being with someone like I feel when I'm with Jim. I don't know if it's because of the trials I've been through or if it's just because it's different. You ask a hard question, and I don't know if I can truly give you an answer. I do like him an awful lot. I like being around him, and I like how I feel when I'm around him. He makes things so much fun."

"I see," said Andrea.

"Anyway, I was wondering if you could help me. I want to get Jim something for Christmas, but I don't know what to get him."

Andrea was thoughtful for a moment. "Well, how much money do you want to spend, and how personal do you want the gift to be?"

"I don't know. That's why I'm calling you."

"Okay, let's tackle the first issue. How much money do you want to spend?"

"I could certainly spend 100 dollars on him."

"Well, Susan, for most men, their hearts are won through their stomachs. But with men like George and Jim, you need to add something else. You not only win their heart through their stomachs but also by buying them something for hunting. You never fail when you do that."

"Oh," Susan breathed. "What does he need? What would he like to have?"

"He needs a bi-pod for the front of his rifle. I got one for George last year for Christmas, and Jim has been bugging him about it ever since. He wishes he had one. You couldn't go wrong with that. A good one will cost 70 dollars."

"I wouldn't know where to buy it around here. Where would I go?"

"Leave it to me," Andrea replied. "You write a love note to Jim and send it to me. I'll get the present, put your note inside, wrap it up for him and tell you how much it cost."

"You've always been my friend, Andrea," said Susan, "and now I definitely know why."

Chapter 16

It was the Sunday evening before Christmas, and Jim was in Pastor Burns' office. In half an hour, the business meeting of the church would begin and the congregation would have to come to a decision about how to receive into their fellowship an elderly man who had just served twenty years in prison.

"How do you think it will go?" Pastor Burns asked Jim.

"There's only one way it can go," replied Jim.

"I agree, but I pray that God will give us the wisdom to help everyone in the congregation to see it that way as well."

Jim and Pastor Burns left the office and went into the sanctuary. They were amazed at how many people had come to the church. Indeed, this was a topic of interest, and it needed to be addressed thoughtfully.

Pastor Burns opened the meeting with prayer, and the music minister led the congregation in singing a couple of gospel songs. When the songs had concluded, Pastor Burns invited the leader of the pastors' council, the leader of the church council, and Jim to come forward. Together, they stood side by side before the congregation.

"We're here," Pastor Burns began, "to determine how we can best protect our friend who will be back with us in another month. We're here to protect the congregation.

We're here to protect the gospel of Jesus Christ. We're here to protect each other. The pastors' council, the church council and the ministerial team of the church have met and discussed, at length, the ramifications of what we as a congregation are required to do in the days ahead. We believe that we are all sinners who have been saved by grace. We believe that sin is sin, and that while without doubt some sins can seem worse than others, all disobedience to God is sin. We believe our friend was reformed prior to his prison sentence and, even though he has spent twenty years behind bars, he has kept and maintained his faith. His offenses occurred many, many years ago. He has asked for forgiveness, and God has forgiven Him. God no longer even remembers his sins. As a congregation, we can do no less.

Pastor Burns paused for a moment before continuing. "However, for the peace of mind of the people within our congregation, we need to decide how we can be comfortable and worship together. We also need to protect our friend from those who, out of spite or fear, would try to derail him and find ways of getting rid of him by putting him back into prison on the charge of a repeat offense. For this reason, we've prepared a PowerPoint presentation to give you some of the guidelines that we've established. For some, these guidelines may seem as though they are based on a cruel joke or a total lack of trust. For others, they may not seem strict enough to gain adequate protection. But again, I would call us all to remember that we're all God's children and that all of us are saved by grace. We are all sinners and have done things in the past that we wouldn't want others to know about. It just so happens that we know the ugly past of our brother. We want him to feel comfortable in coming to church. Now, the four of us who stand before you will try to answer your questions and listen to the comments that you may have."

The meeting went on for an hour as they discussed and hashed out the pluses and minuses of allowing the brother back into the fellowship. As the meeting progressed, Jim was impressed with the spiritual growth that he saw in most of the people. Many more than before were now willing to extend forgiveness to the man. There were still a few people for whom Jim felt extremely sad—those who said they would be afraid to be around someone with such a background and couldn't find it in their hearts to forgive. *If these people knew everything in everyone else's past, where would they go to lead safe lives?* he wondered. *How would they survive? Each one would be a nervous wreck. And yet, they, too, were sinners saved only by grace.*

Jim's heart hurt for a couple of families in particular who threatened to leave the church. He didn't want anyone in the congregation to feel that they needed to take such dire action. He smiled at those who stood up to say that just as there were those who would leave if it was decided to let Ernest come to church, there were many more who would leave if the gentleman wasn't allowed to come to church.

At the close of the meeting, Pastor Burns announced that between the extended church family and the parole board, lodging had been found for Ernest where he would have a home and be protected. Jim was glad that this was one area that wouldn't have to be worked out among the congregation.

Later, back in the pastor's office, Pastor Burns asked the three men how they felt the meeting had gone. They just stood there and looked at each other with thoughtful expressions on their faces. None was quick to speak. Finally, Jim said, "I believe we have a congregation of Christians in which some eat meat and some are still sucking on a bottle." The others also murmured their agreement.

"Well, we are all at different levels in our Christian growth," Pastor Burns said. "As leaders of our church, we need to help each person grow into a deeper, closer and more meaningful relationship with Jesus Christ."

Driving home, Jim was jolted by the realization that Christmas was only a few days away. He had bought George and Andrea presents, he had presents ready to ship to Sam and Martha in Pennsylvania, and he had presents for his parents. But what should he do for Susan? Should he send her a present? If so, how personal a present should it be? Jim touched a button to activate the voice-command on his cell phone and said, "Call Andrea."

Andrea had just arrived home from the church meeting when she answered the call. "What's up, Jim?" she asked.

Jim's simple reply was, "Help!"

"Help what?"

"I need help."

"I thought that most of the congregation responded well this evening, so I don't believe that's why you're asking for help," Andrea stated. "Do you have a flat tire? Is that the type of help that you need?"

"No," said Jim. "It's about Christmas. I've gotten my parents' presents, I've gotten your presents—don't tell yourself or George—and I've gotten Sam and Martha's presents. But there's a young lady that I need to get something for. Help!"

"And when do you assume you'll give this present to her?"

"I don't know. She said that she would be here during New Year's, but I hate to wait that long. What do I get her?"

"What do you want to give her?"

"I don't know. Never in my life have I been in such a position where I want to get a present that matters this much."

"Thanks a lot. And here I thought I was special."

"You know what I mean. I'm talking about getting a present for someone who is in the playing field."

"Give me until tomorrow evening," said Andrea, "and let me see what I can come up with."

"Thanks," Jim replied. "I'll talk to you tomorrow evening." He hung up his cell phone.

"What's going on?" George asked Andrea when she put the phone back down.

"Lover Boy wants to know what to get his darling for Christmas," Andrea replied with a laugh.

"Buy her a hunting license. Buy her a gun!"

"George! That's not what you get a lady for Christmas. Especially not on the first Christmas."

"Well, it seems practical to me." George flipped on the TV to watch the rest of the Sunday night football game.

"Men," Andrea muttered as she went back to their bedroom. She picked up the phone and called Susan.

"Oh, Andrea," said Susan, "it's good to hear your voice. Do you have everything ready for the Christmas present?"

Andrea laughed. "I have your 50 percent ready."

"What do you mean my 50 percent?"

"Well, I had to help you. Now it seems I need to help a young man. What's something that a young lady would like for a Christmas present from a young man?"

"Oh, I don't know. I don't need anything."

"George suggested a gun."

"I don't know about that, but I would like to learn to hunt. Andrea, do you think Jim would teach me how to shoot a rifle?"

"I'm sure he would."

"I want to learn," Susan said quietly. She felt a blush on her cheeks, even though no one else was in the room with her.

"Susan, I do believe that you're in love."

"It would be easy to fall in love with Jim, but we need to go slow. We need to ask for God's guidance. But, Andrea, I daydream. I dream about it at night. Do you think God would give me something so special if it wasn't right? Jim's been so good to me this past month. What will he want to get me?" Suddenly, Susan laughed quietly. "Andrea, I said I have everything, but really I don't. In Jim's world, I would need a good pair of hunting boots."

"That's almost personal," Andrea chuckled. "At least it's clothing."

"That's what I need. And if I'm going to go deer hunting with him in a week or so, I would like to have my own boots so I don't have to borrow yours."

"That would be a good present," Andrea said. "Not too personal, but something very practical for you, especially if you're going to enter Jim's world."

Susan giggled. "It's not a foregone conclusion, but our roads are merging."

"So, what are you doing for Christmas?" Andrea inquired. "What is keeping you there in Ohio?"

Susan thought only a moment and then answered, "Nothing, really."

"If you're coming here for New Year's, why don't you come a week early and be here for Christmas as well?"

Susan gave a little gasp. "Would I be intruding? Would I be barging in? Andrea, are you inviting me?"

"Susan, you won't be intruding. You're one of my closest friends. And it would really shake Jim up. Don't tell him—we'll surprise him. You get here on the twenty-third. We'll keep you hidden and then take it from there."

Susan pondered for a moment. "I really have nothing to keep me here in Ohio, and I'm coming anyway. I would so much enjoy being with you and George."

"And Jim?" Andrea asked.

"And Jim," Susan confessed. "Oh, Andrea, you're such a blessing. If I travel on the twenty-third, I could be well rested and refreshed for Christmas Eve. What is Jim doing on Christmas Eve?"

"He normally spends it with his parents, and we usually get together on Christmas Day and exchange presents. We could surprise him. We could have you at his parents' house. Jim has already introduced you to them."

"I'm getting wound up already. Let me get off the phone and start preparing. But I will be there on the evening of the twenty-third. Oh, Andrea, I can hardly wait!"

Andrea said goodbye and hung up the phone. Then she called Jim's cell phone number. "Jim, this is Andrea," she said. "How much money do you want to spend for some special little lady for Christmas?"

"It depends," Jim replied. "What's the scoop?"

"Well, if someone is going to enter your world, it seems to me that she ought to be able to dress appropriately. How about a pair of good, warm, insulated hunting boots?"

Jim pondered the idea momentarily. "Yes, I think that would be fine. It's not real personal, though. And how do I know her size?"

"She wore mine several weeks ago in Pennsylvania and said they fit fine. And, as far as being personal, well, boots aren't very personal, but the perfume you could get to go along with them would make any woman smile."

Jim was quiet for a second. "How do I know what kind of perfume?"

"My Christmas shopping is almost done, so I believe I'll have time to get those things for you and have them wrapped. All you have to do is cough up the money. Why, oh why, do I go through the extra work just to please a cousin of mine?"

"Because you love me, that's why," Jim snorted.

Andrea laughed. "Yes, I do love you, and I also love a little lady who's wiggling her way into your heart."

"It's not really something I planned," Jim said. "It's just happening. I wondered if it ever would happen, and I wonder how real this actually is."

"Enjoy yourself, Jim."

Susan arrived on the evening of the twenty-third after a successful trip from Ohio. She hugged Andrea and whispered, "It's so good to be here again. Does Jim know that I'm here or that I'm coming early?"

"He doesn't suspect a thing."

"I wish I could see him."

"Not until tomorrow evening," Andrea laughed. "I suggest you don't call him, either. You'd give it away."

Susan and Andrea chatted and were enjoying each other's visit when George came home from the grocery store. He went over to Andrea and gave her a big hug and a tender kiss. "I love you, dear," he said. Then, looking at Susan, he remarked with a twinkle in his eye, "You here again? What do you want around here?"

Andrea pinched George and pushed him away. "Men."

George laughed. "I'm afraid somebody's getting hooked and doesn't even know it."

"I am enjoying myself," Susan replied.

"I'm afraid Jim's liable to trip," said George. "His head is in the clouds so bad he can't even see where he's walking."

"Which reminds me, George," Andrea said thoughtfully, "we need to make sure that Jim doesn't get to his parents' house too early tomorrow evening."

"I have to be at work until closing," said George, "but since it's Christmas Eve, we'll be closing at five instead of nine."

"Could you ask him to meet you at the store for something?" Andrea asked. "We need to keep Jim away from his parents'. He doesn't know that Susan is here, and I want to have her at Jim's parents' home when he gets there."

George rolled his eyes and laughed. "Women," he said. He turned and walked into the dining room. "What's for supper?"

"Food," Andrea responded. "In ten minutes. Food."

Susan helped Andrea finish putting the dinner on the table. They heard George talking to Jim on the phone. "Yeah, Jim," he said, "I need your help tomorrow evening at the store, right at five o'clock. I need to move one of the Christmas tree stands so the store is ready, when we open up at six, the morning after Christmas. We'll be closing at five, and I'll only have a couple of women there and no men around. I'd really appreciate it if you could be there, right at five, to help me."

"I don't want to be late for Christmas Eve with my parents," Jim said. "Is it really that important?"

"It won't take any longer than five or ten minutes. So, if you're there at five sharp, you shouldn't be late." George hung up the phone and turned to look at the women. "Why do I let myself get involved in such things?"

"Be happy, George," said Andrea. "The plot thickens. Let's eat."

After they had eaten, Andrea called Jim's mom and told her about Susan being in town and how she wanted to surprise Jim. "Susan is the lady that Jim introduced to you when we got back from Pennsylvania," she said. "You know, the one who went hunting with us."

"I would love to be able to help her with preparing their Christmas meal," Susan whispered.

Andrea heard her and commented to Mrs. Black that Susan would like to come after lunch to visit and spend time getting to know them. When it was arranged, Andrea got off the phone and turned to look at Susan. "You have a big afternoon and evening ahead of you tomorrow."

Susan grinned. "I can hardly wait. I've met Jim's parents, but I've not really had a chance to get to know them."

"You will by tomorrow at this time," Andrea said. "They're a dear couple, and their son isn't too bad, either."

Susan smiled a sheepish grin. "I haven't seen too much to discourage me," she admitted.

Chapter 17

The next day right after lunch, Andrea took Susan over to the Blacks'. The four visited for a while, and then Andrea left. "I'll see you late tonight," Andrea said. "I assume someone will bring you home."

"I certainly hope so," Susan answered.

Andrea had the early afternoon to finish her Christmas shopping. She needed to drop Jim's wrapped gift to Susan and Susan's wrapped gift to Jim off at the Blacks' and slip them underneath the Christmas tree. She chatted with Susan and Mrs. Black a bit before leaving. "Jim is going to be so surprised," she said.

Mrs. Black laughed. "You need to get him on video when he comes in this evening," she suggested.

"How can we do that?" Susan asked.

"I have an idea," said Andrea. "George and I need to go to my parents' tonight, but if George is holding Jim at the store for a little while, I could be here and then meet him at my parents' house." Andrea picked up her phone and told George what she wanted to do.

George listened and shook his head. "Women," he muttered.

"And you love us to pieces, too," Andrea said.

George grinned and hung up the phone.

Jim met George at the store a little before five, still wondering what was so important that it had to be moved before opening the day after Christmas. George showed him a heavy table that had some Christmas wrappings, decorations and last-minute novelty items on it for impulse buyers. "I want to clear this away so I can be prepared for the next phase of the grocery business," George said, trying to make it sound important. Jim looked at the heavy table and the knick-knacks on it. "I just need to get a grocery cart and pile all of the items in it."

Hardly anybody was in the store when George and Jim set to work. They quickly cleared the table and carried it to the back of the store where the stock was kept. "We'll put it against the wall for now," said George. "I'll think about what to do with it when I come back after Christmas. We'll just leave the items in the buggy." George grabbed Jim's hand and shook it, "Thanks, buddy, and Merry Christmas."

George stayed behind to close the store for the evening while Jim hurried toward his parents' house. He was still wondering what was so all-fired important over getting a table removed from the front of the store. His mind quickly turned to Susan. Tonight he would tell his parents more about her. Maybe this would be the last Christmas that he would have to spend alone. He wished that somehow she could be here so they could spend Christmas together.

A sadness came over him, and he wished that he had asked Susan to come earlier. However, his spirits brightened as he pulled into his parents' driveway "This is a mighty good place to be on Christmas Eve," he said to himself. He stopped the car, opened the back door and took out the presents for his parents. His mind was in a whirl. It was Christmas again, and he was here with his parents. It was a good time of year. Life was good.

He opened the door and walked inside. His mom and dad were right there eagerly awaiting his arrival. "Here, let me take your presents, Jim," his dad offered. Jim looked at them and then saw a blanket hanging in the corner of the kitchen.

"What's that?" he asked.

"Christmastime's a-comin'," his mom sang out. "Stand right there. I think we have an early present for you." Jim wondered what his mom was trying to do. As he waited, his eyes scanned the dining room table, and he saw four places set instead of three. About that time, from around the corner he heard, "Surprise!" Susan stood in the doorway.

"What? How? Where? When?" Jim exclaimed. He rushed forward, and Susan moved to meet him. He gave her a big hug and kissed her on the forehead. Then he looked at his parents and at the blanket. A look of consternation came over his face. He strode over to the blanket. There was a small hole cut into it. Jim pulled the blanket back and threw up his hands in exasperation. "Andrea, what are you doing here?"

"Running the video camera," Andrea answered. "Well, somebody needed to."

Jim looked at her and made a face. He swung back to Susan. "Oh, Susan," he said. All at once, he realized that his introduction of Susan to his parents had been rather brief when they had returned from hunting in Pennsylvania. "Dad, mom, this is Susan," he said. Turning to her, he said, "But how did you get here? What is going on?"

"Surprise!" Susan exclaimed. "I spent a lovely afternoon with your parents. We're already quite well acquainted."

"Who concocted all of this?" Jim asked. Nobody said a word. Jim glanced back at Andrea. "Turn that video camera off, will you?"

"Oh, when I get around to it," Andrea said. "Oh, all right. It looks like it's about time for me to get to my own parents' house anyway."

"Yes, I think as much," Jim replied. He went over and pulled on the blanket. He looked back at Susan. "You're here. Did you get my present I sent you?"

"No. Did you send me a present? That was so kind and sweet of you."

Jim looked at Andrea, a questioning look on his face.

"I told you, Jim, that she would have her present by Christmas Eve. My guarantee stands. We'll see you all later. We've got Christmas at my folks' house this evening."

Jim looked at her, gawking, as she walked out the door. Susan laughed. "Jim, it's so good to see you," she said. She gave him a hug as he turned back to her.

Jim looked at his parents and shook his head. He was at a loss for words. Finally, he blurted out, "Goodness, I'm hungry! When do we eat?"

"Now," Mama Black said. "Now."

They held hands around the table, and Mr. Black said a prayer of thanksgiving for Christmas, for friendships, for loved ones and for the world. They all ended the prayer with a hearty, "Amen." After the prayer, Jim didn't let go of Susan's fingers. "I can't believe you're here," he exclaimed. "How did you get here early?"

"Andrea said to come a week early," Susan replied. "She said they had a bedroom for me in their home. There was nothing to keep me in Ohio, so here I am."

"Chalk one up for Andrea," Jim remarked. "I knew that favorite cousin of mine was good for something." They all laughed and began to eat their Christmas meal.

When the meal was over and the dishes were done, the family moved to the living room. "It is a special time of year," Mr. Black began, looking at Susan, "and we are thrilled and delighted that you can share it with us. In fact, we usually hand out gifts to each other at this time, and I do believe that there's a gift here for you from my wife and me. We'd be honored if you were to open it."

Susan stared at them. "You didn't know I was coming until yesterday."

Mrs. Black smiled. "It doesn't take long to get things done when you have your mind set on it," she said.

Susan was dumbfounded as they put a package in her hands. Mr. Black went back underneath the tree and pulled out another package. "Here's one for me from my son, Jim," he said. "And here's one for Jim from . . . Susan?"

Jim jerked his head up. He watched his dad bring the package to him. "You brought me something?" Jim asked.

"Shouldn't I?" beamed Susan, her eyes sparkling.

"Here's one for me from Jim," said Mrs. Black.

All of a sudden, Susan blushed and a mortified look came over her face. She had made sure that Jim's present from her was there, but she had totally forgotten about getting something for his parents. Mrs. Black saw her expression and realized what was going through her mind. She went over, stood beside Susan and whispered, "Your presence here this afternoon and this evening, Susan, has been a gift far more valuable than money could buy. We're so pleased to have you here. We love you." Tears glistened in Susan's eyes, and she wiped them away with her fingers.

". . . and here's one for Susan from Jim," Mr. Black said.

Susan glanced up with a look of surprise on her face. Jim was startled as well, and then he realized the guarantee that Andrea had given him. "How long did Andrea know this was going on?" Jim asked, turning to Susan.

"Oh, three or four days."

"That cousin of mine is quite a lady."

"Yes, she is, she's my closest friend . . . almost."

Jim looked at her with a twinkle in his eye. "I like the 'almost' part, especially if I know who 'almost' is."

"I believe, Susan, that you should go first," Mr. Black said.

Susan looked at the present from Jim's parents in her hands. "I don't know what to say," she said.

"Dig in, tear off the wrappings, and then say, 'Yippee!'" Mr. Black suggested.

Susan laughed and pulled the wrapping off of the box. Inside was a lady's camouflage coat. Jim looked at it and marveled. "How did you know . . ."

Jim's dad cut him off. "You're twenty-seven years old, and you've never been able to figure out my intelligence network. Don't start now."

Susan stood up and walked over to Mama and Papa Black and gave them each a big hug. "Thank you. I will get to use this next weekend. You're so kind and sweet. Thank you."

More gifts were opened, and then the time came for Jim to open the package from Susan. He looked at the gift and then at Susan. "What can this be?" he said.

"Tear it open and say, 'Yippee!'" Jim's dad suggested again.

Jim tore it open. It was a bi-pod for his rifle. "Wow," he said. "For a city gal, you sure get educated fast."

"Never underestimate my intelligence network," Susan remarked. She smiled and looked at Mr. Black.

"Don't look at me," Daddy Black said to Jim. "I wouldn't tell you anything anyway."

Jim got up and went over to Susan. "I need to give you a hug for this," he said. Instead of going back to his chair, he sat down beside her on the couch.

There was one last present to open, and that was Jim's gift to Susan. She looked at the present, and then looked at Jim. "Oh Jim," she whispered. He sat beside her with a smile on his face that reached from ear to ear. He wasn't sure how she would respond, but with his parents giving her a big, heavy camouflage coat, he somehow felt better about the boots. He watched as Susan opened the package. She looked up at him, and when he looked into her eyes he read volumes. "Oh, Jim, what have you given me? You're so thoughtful."

Mr. Black laughed. "It looks to me like we're making a country girl out of a city girl."

Susan smiled. "I don't think the city girl is complaining." She ran her hand down into the boot to feel how warm and soft it was, and then ran her hand down into the other boot. Her fingers ran into a knot in the toe. Puzzled, she pulled it out. "What is this?" she asked.

"It looks like a toe-stuffer," Jim humorously remarked.

Susan pulled the wrappings off and saw her favorite perfume. "Oh, Jim, how did you know?" She leaned over and gave him a peck on the cheek, and then felt very self-conscious. She looked at Mr. and Mrs. Black. "You all have been so kind. Jim has been so kind, and if this continues to go the way that it's going, I will be able to enjoy and love a family again."

Mrs. Black got up and came over and hugged Susan. "Let's just keep trusting and praying," she whispered. "But we're thankful God is working in our lives."

Susan smiled. She looked back at Jim and, taking the lid off the perfume bottle, turned it up on her finger and dabbed a little behind her ears.

"Smells good enough to eat!" Jim responded.

"You can't be hungry," his mom said.

"Another piece of pie wouldn't hurt," Jim teased.

"I second that," Mr. Black said. He watched the women get up and go to the kitchen. "We could get it," the men offered in unison.

"You could, yes," Susan came back, "but I'm happy to do it for you."

Mr. Black looked at Jim. "She's quite a lady, son."

"Yes, Dad, she's quite a lady. We've only known each other for a month, but it seems like I've known her all of my life."

Mr. Black smiled. "Keep praying, keep observing and keep asking God for direction, son. Your mother and I have been extremely impressed today with the young lady who has crossed your path. We've learned a lot about her this afternoon, and your mother and I are at peace."

Jim went over and gave his dad a hug. "Thanks, Dad, for my upbringing and your affirmation. I think I'm the most blessed man alive."

"We're all blessed," his dad agreed. "Just keep pursuing God as you pursue Susan and God will reveal His plans for you."

The women came back with the pie. The rest of the evening was spent with games, fellowship, laughter and love. Finally, Jim looked up at the clock on the wall. "Mercy, it's 11:30 already," he said. "It's time for us to go home." He looked at Susan. "Are you ready to go to Andrea and George's?"

Susan smiled an affirmative. He and Susan told his parents goodbye, and then they took their presents out to Jim's Jeep. As Jim drove to George and Andrea's home, he said, "This has been the best Christmas ever."

Susan smiled. "Yes, this Christmas has been very special, and I am looking forward to what's coming next. I believe we're getting together with George and Andrea tomorrow, on Christmas Day."

"Yes," Jim said. "I know that I need to leave you with George and Andrea, but I really wish that we wouldn't have to be parted."

Susan looked at Jim and took his hand. "That would be nice. I would like that, at the right time and in the right place." She gave Jim's hand a squeeze. "I'm amazed at how blessed we are and that God has worked to bring us together. I certainly am looking forward to the next week."

When they reached George and Andrea's house, Susan looked at Jim, her brown eyes smiling, and said, "I have a request for you, Jim."

"And what would that be?" Jim asked.

"I want you to help me shoot a deer rifle before we go hunting."

Jim looked at Susan with a look of astonishment on his face. "That would be fun. I would love to help you learn how to shoot. But why the rush? Why now?"

Susan squeezed Jim's hand harder. "I thought, maybe, that you would help me shoot a deer in the next several days."

Jim's heart leaped. To have a spouse who would share the sport that he loved would be a tremendous blessing. "But, Susan, it would take $130 to buy a hunting license that you could only use a couple of days, because then the deer season would be over. Would that be realistic for you to do that? That's a lot of money."

Susan responded with another squeeze of the hand. "Yes, Jim, that's my Christmas present to me. I can afford to do that. I don't throw money away, but this is special, and I want very much to enjoy doing this with you."

Jim took a deep breath. "After we have lunch tomorrow, we can go out and get started."

"I would like that," Susan replied. "And by the way, thank you for my boots."

Jim laughed. "What a Christmas present! Thank you for my bi-pod."

"I want to see you make a long shot—say, 400 yards?"

Jim laughed again. "It could happen. I've done it before."

Susan let go of Jim's hand and started to open her door. Jim quickly jumped out of the Jeep, ran around to the passenger side, opened the door, and then helped her up to the house. "Is the door locked? Are George and Andrea here yet?"

Susan laughed. "I didn't even consider the fact that they might not be here, and Andrea didn't give me a key." Jim tried the door, but it was locked. He walked over to the garage and checked. He could see in the dim light that the car was not in the garage.

"Now what?" Susan asked.

"Well, I could take you to my place. That's what I would like to do, but that wouldn't be appropriate or look proper."

Susan smiled. "No, it wouldn't." Just then, they heard a car and saw lights in the lane. "Good timing," Susan said.

They waited until George and Andrea opened their doors. Jim gave Susan a hug and a kiss on the cheek. "Until tomorrow," he said.

"Until tomorrow," Susan said, and gave him a hug back. "Oh, Jim, I am so glad to be here. It seems like the last couple of weeks have been forever. I could hardly wait to get back here and hold you."

"I must admit that I rather like it myself," Jim said.

Susan let go and gave him a shove. "Be off with you. I'll see you tomorrow."

"Tomorrow," Jim replied, a big smile on his face. He waved to George and Andrea, turned and jumped into his Jeep, and drove home.

As Jim drove, his mind was in a whirl. He could hardly contain himself. He thought back over the evening—the surprise of having Susan there, the joy of being with her, the way his parents had accepted her, the thrill of holding her in his arms . . . "What's next, God?" he pleaded. "Oh, I want what You want, but would You have this happening if it wasn't to be?" Jim thought about teaching her to shoot a rifle. He had a .270 rifle that he normally used, but he had started off with a 6mm, which was a lighter rifle. It would be perfect for Susan to use, he had plenty of shells for it, and it was sighted in. He would have fun tomorrow helping her learn how to shoot.

It was past 12:30 when Jim got home and went to bed. Although it was late, he lay awake for a long time dreaming about Susan and the life that they might share together one day. He tried to step back, think rationally and look at the pros and cons, but finally he gave up. "Lord, in the end, I realize that I just need to seek You and Your love first and trust You to lead me in this situation," he whispered. "Oh, God, I really think Susan might be the woman for me. Please, Lord, guide my footsteps.

As Susan, George, and Andrea walked into the house, Susan said, "Merry Christmas, you two."

"Merry Christmas to you, Susan," Andrea said. "How did your evening go?"

"It couldn't have been better. Oh, Andrea, I am so thankful that I'm here."

George, hearing the comment, smiled. "I can't sing too well, so don't ask me to sing for the Big Day."

"Wouldn't it be nice if there was to be a Big Day?" Susan countered. Then she said to Andrea, "Could I talk with you for a moment in the bedroom?"

"Sure," Andrea said. She called back to George, "I'll be there in a minute," and followed Susan to the bedroom.

Once there, Susan turned and said, "Oh, Andrea, I can't believe all the wonderful things that are happening. I'm so excited I just don't know which way to turn. I just can't fathom how I feel. I would say it's as good as Christmas, but this *is* Christmas—and it's all wrapped up with Christmas. I never knew that Christmas could be so good."

"The life you had before, Susan, wasn't that good?" asked Andrea.

"What my first husband and I had was wonderful, but I've never felt or experienced anything like this before."

"Has he popped the big question yet?"

"No, but he's been making innuendos."

"Has he kissed you?"

"On the cheek. Jim said he didn't want to kiss my lips until he knew that we were to be together."

"There's nothing wrong with that," Andrea remarked. "I think he's a real gentleman, and I, without a doubt, know that you're a lady. When y'all are out there deer hunting and you shoot a deer, you may just have to grab him and pounce on him and give him a big ol' smooch."

"Oh, go on!" Susan laughed. "He should take the initiative. But seriously, Andrea, I've been in what I thought was love before, but this is so much more. I love that man. My whole life could be here. I first laughed when I pictured myself as a minister's wife, but the more I think about it, I think I could be a real helpmate for Jim. I could help with visitation, do some volunteer work at the church—I don't have to make an income. We could raise a family. ... Oh Andrea, I'm so overjoyed I can hardly contain myself."

"Sleep tight, lady, sleep tight." Andrea turned and went to her own bedroom and to George.

The next five days went by quickly. With Jim's training, Susan could shoot his rifle like a pro. Maybe she couldn't get a shot off as fast as an experienced hunter could, but she was showing remarkable marksmanship. She spent time with Jim in his home, and he spent as much time with Susan as he could. Before they knew it, they were easing into a ground blind for their first hunt together.

Jim, Susan, George and Andrea had arrived at a friend's farm the evening before, and Jim was eager to show Susan where they would be sitting during the hunt. They had gotten to the blind just as the morning sky was starting to display streaks of pale pink in the east. It was a small hut-like structure that was big enough for two people. Jim had harvested numerous deer from this exact spot in previous years, and he was hoping that it would deliver again on this special day.

Susan looked at Jim with girlish delight and said, more loudly than she had planned, "Okay, we're hunting now!" Her childlike expression of awe and enthusiasm, though evident in her tone of voice, was lost in the dim morning light.

"Not yet," Jim whispered, as a tradesman would teach his eager apprentice. "It's too dark to see."

Susan elbowed him. "You know what I mean. I'm so excited. Do you think we'll see any deer?"

"Well, I certainly hope so," Jim smiled. "We need to be quiet, though. The less noise and movement we make in the woods, the better off we'll be."

They sat together, shoulder to shoulder. Susan reached over and picked up Jim's hand and held it in her lap. Daylight snuck up on the darkness, bullied it away and proclaimed its dominance to the morning. The woods were quiet. They were looking out over the edge of a cow pasture, the woods and another small clearing. The woods served as a funnel between the deer feeding and bedding areas on the farm.

"Look," Jim whispered.

"There's a deer!" said Susan. "Can I shoot it?"

"No," Jim replied. "It looks like two fawns, and we don't have to kill fawns. I'd like for your first deer to at least be a mature doe, if not a buck."

Susan was breathing hard. Jim looked over at her. Her variegated brown eyes were alive with excitement. He looked into their depths and almost forgot that he was deer hunting. "I can trust you, Jim," she said, "to make the right decision."

Jim looked at her, again, and the enormity of that statement hit him. "Just in deer hunting?" he asked quietly.

"In life," Susan answered, also in a quiet whisper. She was thankful that the wrap she had on covered her neck and ears, as she felt them quickly become very hot. Yet the statement she had just made was true, and it spoke volumes.

Jim continued to look at her with a smile on his face. "You are some girl," he said. "Okay, let's find you a deer." They turned back and watched the two fawns as they slowly fed through the narrow stand of trees. "Here comes another one," Jim said. "It's much bigger. It's a doe. You can shoot that one."

Susan worked to get her rifle propped just right on the shooting sticks. The deer kept walking. Susan looked for it in her scope, but she was having trouble finding it. Jim blew on his doe call, and the deer stopped momentarily and looked in their direction. "Shoot it," Jim whispered.

Susan continued struggling to find the deer in her sights. Finally, she found the creature in her scope and got it lined up. In that same instant, the doe flipped up its tail and bounded away.

"Wait," Jim whispered, in a half-whisper and a hiss.

Susan looked at him with disappointment on her face. "I messed up," she said.

"You didn't mess up; you just aren't experienced in the ways of hunting. It takes time and practice. You'll be okay. You'll do fine."

"Do you think I'll get another chance?"

Jim smiled. "Over the next couple of days, yes, you'll get another chance."

"But I kept you from shooting one, too. I'm afraid I'm messing up your hunting."

Jim looked at her and grinned. "This is the best hunting I've ever done."

Susan felt reassured and marveled at the kindness of the man whom she sat beside.

"Get ready," Jim suddenly whispered, "here's another chance." He saw that it was a yearling buck, but he didn't say anything. Susan worked to get the deer in her scope, and this time she was able to find it. Jim grunted softly and the deer stopped and looked at them. "Put the crosshairs on the shoulder and squeeze," Jim said barely audible.

The roar of the gun inside the blind was deafening, and the recoil knocked Susan back so that she lost sight of the deer. Jim let out a war whoop. She had shot a little high and hit the deer in the backbone, dropping it in its tracks. The deer was dead before it even hit the ground.

Susan looked up. "Where is it? What happened? Did I get it?"

Jim turned and grabbed her in his arms. "Oh, Susan," he said, "what a woman!"

Susan was shaking from the adrenalin that was coursing through her body. "Did I get it? What happened? I didn't see what happened at all."

Jim continued to hold her, his face close to hers. He kissed her on the cheek and then pulled back so they were looking at each other, face to face. They looked into each other's eyes, Jim feeling the pride and exhilaration of helping Susan and Susan feeling the excitement of all that was happening by being with Jim. Jim continued to look into Susan's eyes, "Oh Susan," he murmured. "What am I going do with you? You are so special."

Susan looked at him with a twinkle in her eyes. "You could kiss me, Jim."

Jim looked at her and felt the impact of what she was saying. His life flashed in front of him—a life of the two of them together. A big smile broke onto his face. "Susan, I'm not saying a word," he said, and then leaned forward and kissed her tenderly on her lips. Suddenly, he pulled back and looked at her. A thousand sparks had flown in all directions. Susan's eyes were closed as if she was dreaming. Jim leaned forward and kissed her again. He carefully sat the rifle on the ground, propping it in the corner of the blind and took her in his arms. "Oh Susan, Susan, Susan, what a woman you are. I'm kissing you. You're kissing me. You know what that means."

Susan gave him a squeeze. "I certainly hope so. I'm taking your word for what it meant."

Jim looked her in the eyes. "I don't believe you'll live in Ohio much longer," he said. "Not if I have anything to do with it. Will you become Mrs. Black?"

Susan pushed him away. "You want me to be Mrs. Black? I'll become Mrs. Black, but you better help me go find Mr. Brown."

Jim laughed, pulled her close and kissed her again. "Let's go find your other deer," he said. "But I think and pray that you found your best dear right now."

Susan responded to the kiss and gave him a hug. "You handsome hunk," she said. "Okay, help me find my other deer."

Jim knew right where the deer lay, and as they drew near to the spot, Susan exclaimed, "It's a buck!"

"Yes, I know," Jim replied. "Your first deer, and a buck at that. It's most likely a year-and-a-half-old six-pointer." Susan knelt down beside the deer and carefully stroked its shoulder with her hand. She touched its face lightly and then its antlers, putting her fingers on each point as she counted them—one, two, three, four, five, six.

"A real trophy, huh?" Jim asked.

"What a trophy," Susan agreed, and then looked up at Jim. "But it's the lesser of the two bucks that I just bagged."

Jim laughed. "I might bag me a doe in a minute here myself. On the other hand, I believe I just bagged me the best doe of all."

Susan laughed. Jim couldn't resist and took her in his arms, hugged her again, and gave her another kiss. The sweetness of kissing someone—someone he loved—was far and beyond his wildest dreams of what it would be like. He brought her head to his chest and held on. "My precious Susan, what a gift God has given me. I want to be the gift to you that you are to me."

"Oh, Jim," said Susan, "what a gift you are. You make my life complete. The paths that I have walked and the happiness that God has brought me . . . oh, Jim, you have no idea how thrilled and humbled and excited I am. I don't think I can live another day without you."

Jim relieved the pressure from the side of her head and let her turn her face up to look at him. He drank in her beautiful eyes and whispered, "Oh Susan, Susan, Susan. What has God done for us?"

"He's brought us together," she said, "and I am so thankful. I love you so much, Jim."

"And I love you." Jim gave her another small squeeze. "Look," he said, "your first deer and it's a buck! Do you think we should get that mounted for you?"

Susan's response was quick. "No, Jim. Let's save the antlers, but let's wait until I get a bigger one—close to what you got in Pennsylvania—and then we'll put that one on the wall."

Jim helped her field dress the deer and take it back to the farmhouse. Later that morning, Susan showed it off to Andrea.

"It's beautiful," said Andrea.

"And it's not the only buck I got this morning," Susan said in a hushed voice.

Andrea turned and looked at her. "Not the only buck? What do you—" In that instant, she saw Susan's radiant eyes and a smile on her face that couldn't be hidden. "Another buck? Would this be a two-legged buck?"

Susan vigorously nodded, not able to suppress her emotion.

Andrea squealed and grabbed Susan. "Oh, Susan," she said, "I'm so happy for both of you! And in a deer blind! How perfectly unique. How just like Jim."

"How just like *me*," Susan corrected. "I caught *him*!"

Andrea continued to hug Susan. "I am so thankful! Oh, what a day this is!"

The women returned to the kitchen, where the men were making sandwiches. Andrea couldn't contain herself. Susan looked at Jim and grinned.

"George," Andrea said, "did you know that Susan got *two* bucks out there this morning?"

"Two?" George was confused. He looked at Jim. "You only brought one in. Where's the second one? What did you all do?"

"Only one was four-legged," Andrea said. "The other one has only two legs."

George looked from Andrea to Susan, saw the blush and the telltale sparkle of Susan's eyes, and then looked at Jim. He was grinning like a 'possum. "Why, Jim, you ornery thing, you. Congratulations!" George grabbed Jim's hand, shook it heartily and thumped him on the back. "So, you got two bucks this morning, huh, Susan?"

"Sure did," Susan laughed. "I shot the one and caught the other."

"I bet he wasn't hard to catch, either," George laughed.

Susan laughed along. "I've been baiting that hook for over a month!"

Jim blushed, gave Susan another hug and kissed her lightly. "I never knew it was so good to get caught," he murmured.

They sat down and began to eat their sandwiches. With the festivities and excitement of the morning, they were all keyed up. The close group of friends had an enriching and grand time of telling tales, of recognizing the goodness of life, and of just being together. They realized the harvest of meat was not nearly the most important topic of the lunch hour.

Chapter 18

Susan finished preparing a meal of cubed steak, mashed potatoes and gravy and green beans. Jim's parents had just driven up into Jim's lane. Jim went out to meet them.

"You're right on time, Pop and Mom," he said. "We're ready to eat."

Jim's parents came into the kitchen. Susan looked up, her face flushed from cooking. They could see the excitement in both Jim's and Susan's eyes. Each wondered what occasion Jim was trying to celebrate in inviting them for this evening meal.

"Let me take your wraps, and let's all sit down at the table," Jim said. "Susan wanted to prepare the meal for you. That way you'll know it's good."

Susan laughed self-consciously.

"We know Susan can cook," Mrs. Black said. "She helped me with our Christmas Eve meal."

They sat down, and Jim asked his dad to give the evening prayer of thanks. That being done, Jim picked up the plate of meat and passed it to his dad.

"Here, Dad, eat up!"

Mr. Black took the plate, held it and looked at Jim and Susan. Instead of helping himself to the meat, he set the whole platter down on his plate. "Okay, what gives?" he said.

"What do you mean?" Jim asked.

"I can see it in your eyes, so spill it. What's going on?"

Jim couldn't contain himself any longer. He stood up, walked behind Susan's chair and, taking her hands in his, said, "Pop, Mom, how would you like to have a daughter?"

Mr. and Mrs. Black rose and came around the table, both exclaiming, "Oh, son . . . oh, Susan!" Jim pulled Susan's chair back, and Susan stood and hugged Mrs. Black. Mr. Black hugged his son. "Well done, son," he said. "I'm proud of you."

"Oh Susan," said Mrs. Black, "what a gift you are. I am so pleased with God's and Jim's choice for a daughter for us. Welcome to our family."

They changed places, with Jim hugging his mom and Mr. Black hugging Susan.

"God is so good," Mrs. Black said.

"Yes, God is so good," agreed Jim.

They stood together for a moment, just looking at each other with tears of joy streaming down their faces.

"This is wonderful," Jim said. "I love Susan with all of my heart. But, quite frankly, I don't want our meal to get cold. Let's eat!"

They all laughed and sat back down at their places. Mr. Black picked up the meat platter and took a few pieces before passing it to his left. The meal and the rest of the evening was a constant buzz of questions and of chit-chat. "When will the big day be?" "What are you going to do?"

"We haven't had time to make all the plans yet," Jim said, looking at Susan. "But, as far as I'm concerned, the sooner the better."

"I certainly agree," Susan replied. "We hope to get married within the next five to six weeks. Jim has been so kind and so sweet. There are still a few things that we want to talk about, but we're so excited we can hardly contain our joy. We wanted you to be some of the first to know.

They talked around the dinner table for a couple of hours. Mr. and Mrs. Black were overjoyed and thrilled at the idea that their family would soon be expanded. Finally, Mr. Black stood and said, "This is nice, but I believe we need to get these dishes done. It's either get up and do the dishes or start eating again!"

Mrs. Black laughed. "That's just what you need, more food! You men get out of the kitchen and let us clean up. We women have a lot to talk about."

After Mr. and Mrs. Black had left, Jim put his arms around Susan. "I believe we have their blessing," he smiled.

Susan snuggled up close to Jim with a tear in her eye. "It's good to think about having parents again. It's good to think about having a husband again. Oh, Jim, it's so good to be loved." She turned, put her arms around him and hugged him tight.

The front of Jim's shirt started to get wet from the tears that were falling from Susan's eyes. Jim just held on and marveled. Kissing the top of her head, he murmured, "Susan, oh, Susan, my Susan."

They stood that way for a minute. Suddenly, a thought struck Jim. "Will you want to work here? Will you need to get licensed in the state of Virginia for nursing? Can you transfer your license from Ohio?"

Susan raised her head and looked into Jim's eyes. "Do I need to work, Jim?"

Jim looked at Susan. "No, you don't need to work. We can make it on my income. We won't be able to live extravagantly, but we will survive."

"No, you don't understand what I mean, Jim. Finances are not a problem. Would it be okay with you if I didn't work? If I spent as much time with you as I could? I could go with you to the hospitals at times to visit the sick, or on home visitations, when appropriate, or to do other volunteer work in the church."

Jim looked at Susan, again. "That would be wonderful," he said. "I don't know what your financial situation is. It's the least of my worries."

"Monetarily, Jim, I'm not what you would call rich, but between the life insurance policies and the inheritance from my late husband and my parents, my income from those sources is adequate without me continuing in my nursing career. We won't be strapped financially."

Jim's eyes met Susan's, trying to comprehend what he was hearing her say. "You mean you don't have to work?"

"Not at all," Susan said. "At least, not to support myself."

Jim was quiet all of a sudden. "I . . . I don't want people to think . . ."

"Jim, you loved me without knowing about my financial situation. It's a non-issue. We'll be able to do some things without being strapped for cash, but I have no desire to live at a high-income level just to show off how the Lord has blessed me. I would give it all away, if necessary, to be with you."

Jim, looking at Susan, shook his head. "What a woman you are."

Susan gave him another hug. "A year ago I never dreamed that I would be delighted to finance a hunting trip for my husband. But now I can hardly wait."

Jim continued to hold Susan, drinking in what she was saying, as the reality of what would be, dawned on him. "Oh, Susan, what can I give you?"

Susan looked up at him with a smile on her face, her starry eyes wide. "You can give me your love," she whispered.

"You have all the love I can give. Oh, Susan, what a life we will have together!"

"What do you want our wedding to be like?" Jim asked Susan the next afternoon. They were on their way back from visiting an elderly man who was in the hospital.

Susan looked at Jim. "I don't have anyone to give me away, and I don't want a big affair. I want to be able to slip into your life quietly and without a lot of fanfare."

"I don't need gifts," Jim said, thinking out loud. "I have all I need."

"I have an apartment at home that's stuffed," Susan added. "But people will want to give us something."

"What if we did the wedding in a way that caught them off guard?" Jim asked.

Susan looked at him with a puzzled expression on her face.

"What if . . ." Jim began, and then outlined briefly to Susan what was on his mind. After he had finished, Susan smiled and said, "That would be funny, but it would be lovely."

"It would be funny for some and downright scandalous for others," Jim laughed. "Do you realize, Susan, there are half a dozen women in our congregation who would jump at the chance to date me in the hope of becoming Mrs. Reverend Black?"

Susan punched him in the ribs. "Oh, how proud you are," she mocked.

"No, seriously," Jim said, "but I haven't given any of them a chance to even start their quest. Susan, none of those ladies, even those in the general church family, have any idea about what has transpired between you and me in the last five weeks."

"I've been to church a couple of times with you," Susan reminded him.

"Yes, but you sat with George and Andrea. And although I was there, you and I being seen together hasn't become an issue. If we do what we're thinking, it will be quite a shock to them."

"It will be interesting to see their reactions," Susan remarked.

Jim pulled out his cell phone and dialed Pastor Burns. The pastor answered on the third ring. "Hi, boss" Jim piped up. "Are you in your office?"

"Sure am. Where are you?"

"Susan and I are coming back from visiting at the hospital. Do you have a few minutes?"

"I have a counseling session an hour from now. How soon can you be here?"

"Give us six or seven minutes. This won't take long, but we want to run something by you."

Pastor Burns looked up from his desk as Jim and Susan walked into his office. He took one look at them and saw the excitement in their eyes. He motioned them over to the chairs. "You might as well sit down and start talking," he said.

"Are we that obvious?" Susan asked in surprise.

"I can normally read people pretty well," Pastor Burns replied. "So let's hear it."

"Pastor," Jim began. "My parents want a daughter." He then hesitated for a moment, and Pastor Burns waited for him to continue. "And I need a wife."

"So, what do you want me to do about it?" Pastor Burns asked, his eyes twinkling.

"With one small ceremony, I think you can accomplish both," Susan said quietly. "I would love to be a daughter, and I would love to be a wife."

Pastor Burns stood and leaned across his desk, grasping Jim's hands. "Congratulations, son. I believe the Lord has worked a good work for you." Turning to Susan, he took her hand and he kissed it lightly on the back. "Congratulations, Susan. I believe that the Lord has given you wisdom."

With the formalities out of the way, Jim laid out the concept that he and Susan were thinking of, regarding the wedding.

Pastor Burns leaned back in his chair and squinted at them. "Have you all thought this out? Is this really what you want?"

"I don't have anyone to give me away," Susan said, "and if we do it this way, we won't have to be concerned about that."

"It will create quite a ruckus," Pastor Burns laughed. "Do you think we can get by with this?"

"Why not?" Jim questioned. "We don't need gifts. If we announce that there will be a catered fellowship meal right after church on a particular Sunday, we can make it a festive occasion. We'll pay for everything. You can tie it in with your sermon, to make the point that you want to make. Our friend from prison will be here next Sunday, and by the time the wedding takes place, he will have been here for more than a month. With your sermon, you can certainly pull it all together."

Pastor Burns got out of his chair. "Give me a second to think," he said. He paced back and forth, his hands to his face and his thumbnails clicking his teeth. "Finally, he stopped in front of his desk. "Are you *sure* this is what you all want to do?"

Jim looked at Susan, and she nodded. "It will be wonderful," Jim answered for them both.

Pastor Burns chuckled. "Yes, it will be wonderful. You'll create quite a stir, and there will be some young ladies who will be highly disappointed, Jim."

"That's totally out of my hands," Jim replied. "They're not the ones to whom God has led me. Susan is God's choice for me."

Pastor Burns laughed to himself. "This could be fun," he said. They chatted for a few more minutes, and then Pastor Burns looked up at the clock on the wall. "I have my appointment in another ten minutes," he said. "You two get out of here and daydream. We'll get together and work out the details regarding that Sunday morning."

Jim and Susan left, hand in hand, and walked to the Jeep. He opened the door and helped Susan inside, then leaned over and put his face close to her ear. "I love you, soon-to-be Mrs. James Black," he said as he kissed her blushing cheek.

"Yes, I'm soon to be Mrs. Black, but my handsome husband-to-be better drive me out of the church parking lot.

Three weeks later, on Sunday morning, Pastor Burns stood before his congregation. It had been a busy three weeks marked with many joys and a few frustrations. The most recent addition to the congregation was present for the second Sunday in a row. The guidelines, a benefit to all, were working and there had been no glitches the previous Sunday or Wednesday night. Ernest was living in a small house in the county and was meeting the state's standards for his freedom. At church, he had a "buddy" with him at all times. He couldn't hurt anyone, nor could anyone accuse him falsely. His probation officer was pleased with the working plan.

As Pastor Burns stood and looked over the 200-plus people, a love welled up inside of him. "Friends," he said, "we have demonstrated God's love over the last two weeks. God is a God of love, a God who wants to heal hurts, a God who wants us to share our life with Him. We, as a congregation, can celebrate God's love. We, as a congregation, can be excited with what God is doing in our midst. We all are human and are sinners who have been saved by grace. Each and every one of us who has accepted Christ as our personal Savior and Lord is a child of the King. From the newborn babies in our church to our oldest members in their nineties, we're growing physically, and we're growing spiritually. I rejoice and am moved when I see people growing spiritually in the Lord. None of us will ever arrive, including myself, until the day we come face to face with our Lord and Savior, Jesus Christ.

"I have been encouraged. In the confines of my office, I have shouted, 'Hallelujah!' I praise God for the way you, the congregation, are growing. Now I think it's time for our church to have a celebration. This will be a celebration of love and of feasting—not of gluttony—but of enjoying good food and good friends, and certainly one of humbleness, extolling the love of our Lord. In saying this, I give notice that two Sundays from today, we will have a fellowship meal immediately following our worship service."

Pastor Burns paused for a moment and looked toward the chairman of the kitchen committee. "The meal will be catered, and special help has been provided to clean up after the meal. If you want to be handy around the kitchen and take care of any needs that may arise, feel free to do so, but your responsibilities of having to do anything in the kitchen will basically be zero. We have a family within our congregation who is anonymously providing the catered meal for this celebration of our church."

Pastor Burns saw the looks of surprise, interest and puzzlement on the peoples' faces. "Let's be content in knowing that we have a lot to celebrate—our family, our love, and our Savior," he said. From there, he went on to his sermon and preached his heart out.

Meanwhile, Susan was back in Ohio, packing her belongings and hiring the movers to bring her life and her possessions to Virginia. The congregation was still not aware of the love saga that would lead to the surprise wedding of their own Pastor Jim.

Chapter 19

The fourth Sunday in February dawned clear and cold. There had been three or four snowfalls throughout the winter, but now the snow was gone and it was cold. However, it was anything but cold in church that Sunday morning. Sam and Martha had come down the day before and had spent the night with George and Andrea. Susan had spent the last few days in the home of her future in-laws. The thrilling sense of expectancy flowed like a charged electrical current, through the friends who knew what was in store.

That morning, when Pastor Burns stood to address the congregation, he said, "It's good to see each of you here today, and it's good that we have a fellowship meal planned after our service. Since you won't need to leave the church to eat, that will give me an extra half hour to preach." There was a smile on his face as he unmistakably heard some muffled groans coming from the congregation. He stopped and asked, "Is that the only response I get?" There was a small ripple of laughter throughout the congregation.

"The sermon today," Pastor Burns began, "is a simple one, but it is a sermon of glory. It is a story of celebration, a story of hope, a story of salvation." For the next half hour, Reverend Burns poured himself into the story of Christ and His Church, explaining to the congregation how, from the abuser to the murderer and from the glutton to the envious, all of us are sinners. He helped the congregation see that when they accepted Christ, they, as a corporate body, became the bride of Christ.

"Marriage is often an illustration used in the Scriptures," Pastor Burns said. He stopped and looked at the congregation. "There are times," he said, "when I use the overhead projector to put up an illustration, but let me see if I can do it a different way this Sunday. I will need some help. Pastor Jim, I can pick on you. It's safe to use you. Please come forward and stand in front of the congregation. Now, let me illustrate marriage to you so that you can draw the parallel as how we, the Christian Body, are Christ's Bride, just as a woman who commits herself to her husband becomes his bride."

Jim stood up from the third row back, walked to the front of the church and faced the pastor. Pastor Burns smiled. "Turn and face the congregation," he said. Jim looked up at him, winked and turned. "Jim will represent Christ," Pastor Burns said. "To continue this illustration, we will next need a bride. Now, before a dozen of you young ladies jump up and come forward to fill in for the illustration, I will confess that we already have a lady picked out."

As he finished the sentence, the back vestibule doors opened and Susan, in a simple white dress, slowly walked up the aisle. People turned their heads, and there were "oohs" and "ahhs" throughout the congregation, followed by a murmur as to who this young lady was and the extreme illustration that Pastor Burns was using. Some people, however, saw the look on Jim's face and the smile on Susan's, and in their minds the realization clicked. Others, intent on the illustration, never comprehended what was actually going on.

Susan stopped in front of Jim, and Jim took her hands. "You two stand facing each other with your backs to the outside walls," Pastor Burns instructed. "Just so you know," he said, addressing the congregation, "this is Susan Handley. She will fulfill the role of bride in our illustration. She is a friend of George and Andrea. In fact, it is customary here to have witnesses, so, to complete our illustration, let's have George and Andrea, if they will, stand beside Jim and Susan. This will complete our wedding party."

Pastor Burns went on to proclaim the rightness and the glory of Christ receiving his Bride and living happily ever after, together. "Christ has laid down some stipulations for us to become His Bride," he said. We have to receive the gift of salvation. It's a free gift. In the same way, I would ask Jim if he's willing to accept the bride that Christ gives him." He looked at Jim. "Do you, Jim, take Susan Handley to be your lawfully wedded bride, to hold, to cherish and to love, until death do you part?"

"I do," said Jim. Looking back at the congregation, he announced, "I will." There was laughter, and a few people raised their eyebrows. More people in the congregation were beginning to understand what was actually taking place.

"Christ decided long ago to accept His Bride," Pastor Burns continued. "He was willing to die to make that provision and, as the male figure in our earthly marriages, the husband is the protector and should be willing to lay down his life for his bride. Do you, Susan, take this man, Jim, to be your lawfully wedded husband, to love, to cherish, until death do you part?"

Susan looked at Jim and said, "I do." Looking back to the congregation, she also said in a loud voice, "I will." She and Jim looked at each other, and the congregation laughed.

"In the end," Pastor Burns continued, "Christ's Bride will finally be gathered to Him, and it will be an earth-shattering experience. When Christ receives the Church, His Bride, they will go on together, victorious forever. They will be united and become one. So, to you, the congregation, I proclaim that by the powers vested in me by the state of Virginia and by God Almighty, Jim and Susan are one. To you, the congregation, I proudly present Pastor and Mrs. Jim Black." Pastor Burns nodded to Jim and said, "And now, Pastor, you may kiss your bride."

The congregation sat in stunned silence, and then whispers started to break out. What was going on? All of a sudden, people began to applaud. It soon became a crescendo of clapping and shouts, with the people rising to their feet as they realized what they had just witnessed.

Pastor Burns held his hands in the air and, after a couple of minutes, order was again restored. "Can you imagine how delighted God in heaven will be when His Son and His Bride are joined together as one, forever?" he asked. "The excitement and rejoicing that will happen then cannot be compared to the small amount of exhilaration and exuberance that you've shown in the last couple of minutes.

Now, to the congregation, let me make some proclamations. Most importantly, let me declare to you, just in case there is any misunderstanding, that in the eyes of the state of Virginia and in the eyes of God, you have witnessed the authentic wedding of Reverend Jim Black and Susan Handley."

"Jim and Susan have known each other for several months, and I have talked to each of them and have watched their love grow. I'm elated for our assistant pastor. Jim and Susan both had established homes, so they did not need presents or showers to get them started in creating a home together. For those who don't know, Susan, our bride, comes from Ohio. For the last two years, she has been a widow. Her previous husband was killed in a car accident. She is a special lady who loves the Lord and is thrilled to have the love of Jim in her life. Of course, Jim, our groom, does not need an introduction to you.

"When Jim and Susan came to me with their plan, at first I had reservations about how they wanted to be married. But the more I thought about it, the more I chuckled inside. To you, the congregation, let me assure you that Jim and Susan love you and will continue to work among you. They are excited to be a part of this church family. And now, it probably makes sense to you as to why we are having a fellowship meal. So let's go and celebrate the marriage of the Lamb. Let's go and celebrate the marriage of Jim and Susan." The congregation erupted in applause again.

"Jim," Pastor Burns continued when the noise had died down, "please take your bride, with your bridal party, to the reception area. Certainly, as guest of honor, you all should go first, and I believe a special table has been set up for you and the family. Now, to the rest of the congregation, let's pray for the noon meal, and then we'll be dismissed."

Pastor Burns prayed a prayer of thanksgiving for Christ, for His Bride and for the church, and then he prayed a special blessing on Jim and Susan. After the "amen" there came yet another round of applause and cat-calls and whistles. A few single ladies were a little annoyed and a little crushed, but no one could deny the joy and the jubilation they saw on the faces of Jim and Susan.

Three hours later, Jim looked at his watch. It was 2:30. He looked at Susan, who was standing beside him, and saw that she had a glow on her face. They had been congratulated by nearly everyone in the church, and there was a festive atmosphere in the air. Pastor Burns tapped his glass, and gradually everyone quieted. Now that he had their attention, he spoke. "Jim and Susan do not need presents, but as the pastor of this church, I took the liberty to give them a present from the church, and I trust the church council will back me in the decision I have made. As a gift from the congregation, we're giving Jim the next week as paid time off from his church duties. If anyone needs anything, I will be here to serve you."

Again, applause broke out, and somewhere in the back of the crowd a voice was heard to say, "Where are you going on your honeymoon?"

Jim looked at Susan. Quietly, he pointed and said, "We're starting out by going south."

Half an hour later, Susan held Jim's hand as they headed north on I-81. She looked at Jim and squeezed his hand. "Jim, we're not going south."

"We did for a while," Jim replied. "I didn't say how far or for how long."

Susan laughed.

"I never dreamed of spending a honeymoon in a hunting cabin," Jim confessed. His eyes twinkled as he turned and looked in her face and then into her captivating brown eyes. "I'm just wondering if I'll have to sleep on the couch tonight."

"If you do, I'll be there with you," Susan giggled.

Jim continued to drive, struggling to keep his eyes on the road while he stole another quick glance at Susan. "Oh, Susan, my wife, my love," he said. "I was wondering, Susan dearest, did you bring any nightlights along?"

Susan laughed. "Come to think of it, I brought two: one for the bedroom and one for the bathroom. I would sure hate to get a black eye on my honeymoon."

Jim laughed. "I certainly trust that we won't let that happen."

They drove on toward Pennsylvania as the sun began to set. But in Jim and Susan's hearts, they both felt as though the sun was rising with the glorious dawn of promise—a promise of life and of love.

About the Author

Dwight Burkholder was born in Harrisonburg, Virginia, the seventh of eight children. He grew up on a small farm where he learned the value of hard work and the importance of family values. Married at the age of 20, Dwight worked for a residential builder where he learned the carpentry trade. An avid hunter, Dwight has hunted extensively throughout the United States and South Africa. Dwight and his wife, Linda, enjoy travel and have visited places such as Europe, Italy, Sicily, South Africa, Mexico, Australia, Fiji and Brazil. The Burkholders are active in their local church in Virginia. They are proud parents of three adult children: Douglas, Latonya, and Susan and delighted grandparents of Reuben Joseph. Dwight's other hobbies include golf, music, and playing the fiddle.

To find out more about Dwight Burkholder and other books that he authors go to:

www.DwightBurkholder.com
or
www.ThePreachersDear.com

You may also contact Dwight through email at:

Info@DwightBurkholder.com